THE WARLOCKS CONQUEST

SHIFTERS OF BLACK ISLE #4

LORELEI MOONE

eXplicitTales

CONTENTS

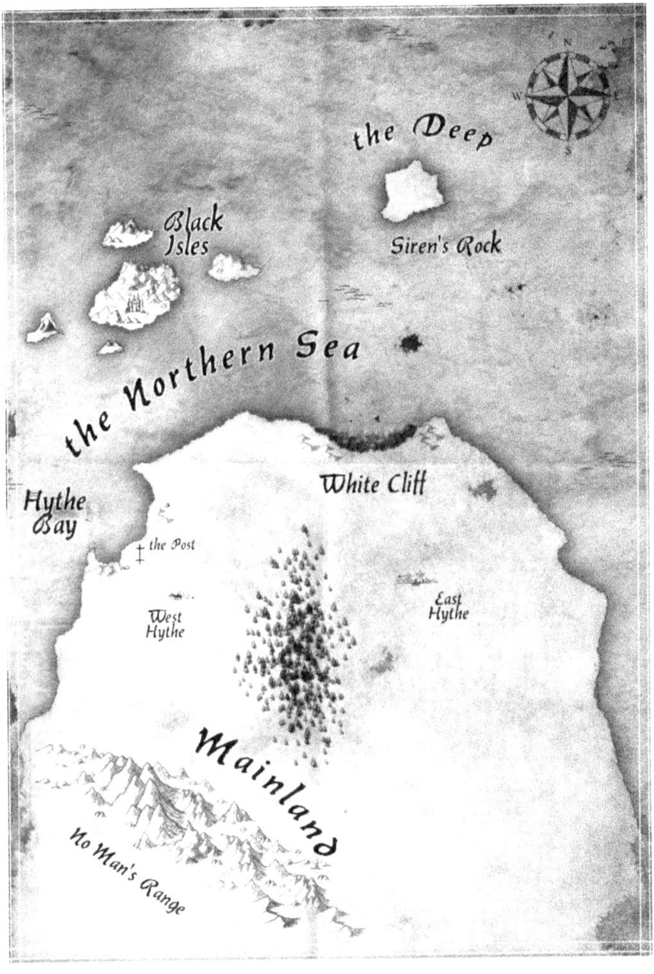

the Deep
Black Isles
Siren's Rock
the Northern Sea
White Cliff
Hythe Bay
the Post
West Hythe
East Hythe
Mainland
No Man's Range
N
S
E
W

PROLOGUE

◆

Once in every eight springs, a girl will be put forth by one of the coastal regions. A peace offering, a condition of the truce between the Giant Warriors of Black Isle and the men of the mainland.

1. No one shall remain with the offering when the time comes.

2. None shall attempt to lay eyes on or follow the giants.

3. No girl shall ever come home, or her village shall feel the giants' wrath.

By this ritual we are bound, so long as our truce may last.

Ferris was free, at least for the moment. After a long nine months at sea, the solid ground underneath his feet gave him a spring in his step he hadn't had in a while.

How he had looked forward to this moment. He'd held onto the fantasy of his return through every storm. Or whenever the work threatened to overwhelm him.

Home at last.

Ferris whistled a cheerful tune as he walked through the village where he had grown up. Of course, his home was still a little distance away on the outskirts of the main settlement, but he could have crossed entire mountain ranges if he had to. Such was his excitement.

"Afternoon," he greeted some of the villagers gathered in the square. These faces had just been a distant memory to him while he'd been away.… The butcher and his wife, the tanner and some younger boys who worked as farm hands stood by in silence as he passed them.

Ferris shrugged and carried on. The villagers had never been too friendly with him or his sister, Kelly, especially since their mother had passed. Things hadn't changed much upon his return, it seemed.

Though *he* had changed a bit; his time at sea had hardened him. Whereas a younger him would have been hurt by their rejection, it no longer mattered to him now. They weren't who he had come back to meet.

As he continued up the path that snaked along the dunes surrounding his family home, he took one final look back. More people had gathered in the square. The news of his arrival was spreading fast.

Ferris chuckled. No matter how quickly gossip spread in this small hamlet, his arrival would still come as a surprise to Kelly. And hers was the face he was most excited to see.

There it was in the distance; the modest home he and Kelly had grown up in. It was smaller than he remembered. Just a little more battered by the elements. Just a little shabbier than it used to be.

But it was still miles better than the accommodation on the merchant ships. Deckhands slept in any space they could find. In between cargo, on the floor. With the cats they'd brought onboard to control the mice and rats. They didn't even have enough blankets between them to keep warm on some nights.

But that was all over for now.

Ferris could hardly contain himself as he reached the front door. He didn't even announce himself as he pushed it open.

But there was nobody inside. He turned around and scanned the fields. Perhaps Kelly was busy out there somewhere, though he hadn't seen her on his way up to the house.

"Kelly?" he called out.

No response.

He checked the inside again. There was something different about the place. The changes were subtle. It was much emptier than he remembered, almost desolate.

No pot of stew bubbling away. The fireplace was cold, as though it hadn't been lit in a while. The baskets where Kelly normally stored the family's supply of potatoes and onions were empty.

"Kelly!" Ferris shouted again. "Father?"

Nobody replied.

It was as though no one lived here anymore. Now, he noticed the dust. The table, the chairs; every last surface was covered under a layer of the stuff.

Ferris dropped the small bundle of his belongings on the floor and ran all the way back down the path. The villagers might not like him, or his family, but they owed him some answers.

What on earth had happened during these nine months he'd been away?

Where was his family?

———◆———

Slumped on one of the chairs of the local tavern, Ferris couldn't do much more than shake his head.

It had taken some time, as well as of threats of violence, to get some of the villagers to open up. The news was worse than he could have imagined.

Kelly had been taken away to the Black Isles by the giants.

He'd been aware of the lottery, of course. Every eight years a village girl had to go. But he never imagined Kelly would get chosen.

What were the chances? He didn't even know this past spring it had been West Hythe's turn to provide an offering.

"How could he let this happen?" Ferris muttered to himself. "And where the hell has *he* gone?"

"Your what?" the bar girl quipped. "Oh, your old man. Don't let it bother ya too much. Mine's run off somewhere too. They get to a certain age and lose their minds. Drinking and gambling is all they can think about. Another?"

She held up the pitcher of ale in Ferris' direction.

He shook his head. "I don't think so."

He picked up the crude stoneware mug and emptied it with one final swig.

As he tried to get up from his seat, he could feel the buzz of the ale starting to hit him, forcing him back down.

But it had done nothing to numb the shock. Kelly was gone. More than one of the people he'd spoken to had tried to hint that she was probably dead by now. Apparently, he shouldn't dwell on the past. Easy for them to say. Kelly wasn't their family, she was his.

And she couldn't be dead.

He wouldn't accept it.

"I won't have it. I won't stand for this."

Ferris balled his fist and slammed it down onto the table. A dull ache pierced his arm all the way up to his elbow. He flexed his fingers a few times, but the pain still remained.

"Now, now. You break the furniture, you pay for it," the girl said.

Ferris shook his head. *Whatever.*

But what was he going to *do* about all this? Would he sail to the Black Isles himself and bring Kelly back? How ridiculous. He was barely eighteen, and although he was tall, he did not have the muscle to match. Plus, they were giants. He would be no match for them.

Nobody in living memory had ever laid eyes on one of them. It wasn't worth the risk, as staying and watching them take away their offering every eight years was punishable by death. But the legends had to be based in truth.

Warriors, they were.

Whereas he was a deckhand.

There was no way he could take the fight to them, at least not now and not on his own.

But he'd-

"In fact, you'd better pay for that ale now as well," the girl interrupted his thoughts.

"What?" Ferris asked.

She pointed down at his empty mug. "How do I know you're good for it, huh?"

Ferris made a face and clumsily checked his pockets for a few coins. He threw them on the table.

"Will that do?" he snapped.

"Thank you very much indeed, sir." The girl smiled as she gathered up the money.

There went a significant portion of his earnings from his time at sea.

But Ferris was least concerned.

He had to think of a way to get Kelly back. Because no matter what anyone said, she was still alive. He could feel it, right there in his chest.

He would have his revenge. This he vowed to himself. Ferris would work day and night to acquire the necessary skills to be able to fight for her honor and her life. If it was the last and only thing he did with his life.

Everyone and everything else could go to hell.

The Warlock's Conquest

Kelly, hang in there. I'm coming for you.

This was the one and only thing on his mind as he stumbled through the village, back to his now empty home.

CHAPTER ONE

* Almost seven years later *

A morning like any other, Eryn was readying herself for her shift. She strapped the rigid leather armor across her chest and tightened a pair of matching cuffs around her wrists. Of course, she'd have to discard these items and more, if she took to the skies in her eagle form. But for time spent on ground, she had come to enjoy dressing like this.

Like a uniform, these items gave her a certain confidence, an air of authority.

For seven years she had performed her duties on Black Mountain under General Rhea's leadership. Ever since Rhea had first enlisted her and the other eagles following the first Sea Folk invasion, she had barely spent a day away from her post.

Luckily the Isles had been at peace for the majority of this period, thanks to the truce that had been negotiated with the enemy under the seas. As a result, these Isles had become a different place than the one she had grown up in. Their peace wasn't so fragile anymore.

The people of Black Isle were flourishing now that they did not have to spend every waking hour preparing for a fight. But while some of the other eagles had gone back home, Eryn had stayed on Black Mountain. She hadn't allowed herself to become complacent.

She'd learned to fight, especially with bow and arrow.

She'd learned to read under Uri the Elder's tutelage, and loved nothing more than to spend time in the library, studying up on strategy and science alike.

No longer the simple farm girl she had grown up as, Eryn was now a fully-fledged member of Rhea's army and often acted as Rhea's right-hand woman. And there was no point in wasting these hard-earned talents by tending her parents' land. Plenty of people could do that in her stead.

Eryn had come to enjoy her duties, so it was with a spring in her step that she joined Yorrick, head of the Castle Guard on the fortifications surrounding the castle.

"Morning. Anything to report?" Eryn asked.

"All quiet. Just as quiet as yesterday and the day before."

Eryn stole a glance in his direction. She couldn't tell if he thought that was a good or a bad thing.

"Better than the alternative," Eryn remarked.

"Sure."

Eryn shrugged. He was a man of few words, and seemingly even fewer emotions, which was fine by her. These qualities made him easy company while on duty.

She made her way back down the fortified wall and headed toward the armory. The lookout squad was already assembled inside. All of them were eagles like her, but in many ways they were not alike at all.

There was a reason she had emerged as their leader.

"Ready?" she asked.

They shrugged and grumbled words of reluctant agreement. This was just a chore to them, a job like any other. Like cogs in a machine, they seemed unaware of the bigger picture. Of just how important their role was in the overall defense of these lands.

Still, they turned up every day and did as they were told, so there was no real reason to complain.

"You know the drill. Immediately let me know if you see anything out of the ordinary."

"What's the point? Nothing ever happens," one of the younger males complained.

"Be grateful for that, as long as it lasts. If you don't remember for yourself, ask your elders what happened the last time we were attacked," Eryn snapped.

The boy responded with nothing but a silent stare.

He was somewhat right, of course. Nothing had happened in all these years. Eryn could only hope their peace would remain.

She watched them leave in clusters of two or three, and followed the last group. Eryn was still on their heels as the lookouts made their way through the winding corridors of the castle toward the View Point, a high plateau that could be accessed from one of the turrets. High above the crashing waves surrounding the island, it was the ideal place for them to set off.

One by one, each of the men and women threw themselves over the edge and transformed. Deafened by the high winds, Eryn could barely make out the sound of their feathered wings, flapping overhead as they circled once or twice before making off in opposing directions.

They all knew the drill. Where to patrol, how long for, and when to report back. She had trained them well, all things considered.

She paused for a moment, watching them get smaller and smaller before disappearing on the horizon, then she headed back inside.

On days such as these, with neither a hunting party nor Council meeting in the works, there was very little for her to do until her squad of lookouts returned. Yet she wasn't planning to stay idle. Instead she would spend this morning in the library with the Elders, as she had done so many times before.

No matter how much she read, she hungered for more. There was still a wealth of knowledge out there, if you were willing enough to seek it out.

———— ◆ ————

Ferris stood at the helm of his ship, with his hands planted squarely on his hips. The Black Isles were within view, though at this distance they were hardly more than a dark outline against the light gray skies. This was the closest he had been to Kelly in all these years.

After more than six years of preparation, the moment of reckoning was upon him. With King Harrold's support, he'd been able to mount his campaign. A ship and a group of men of his own were part of the deal.

On this very ship, he would bring Kelly back home.

For the rest of the fight, there was the full might of the King's navy to count on, which should not be far behind them.

Ferris had fought, cheated and stolen his way out of the simple circumstances he was born into. He'd understood quickly all those years ago that nothing in this world ever came easily.

A deckhand no longer, Ferris had chosen a different path for himself. One of blood and vengeance.

Getting ahead meant taking matters into his own hands. There were no handouts, especially not for outcasts like him. He wasn't proud of some of the things he'd done to get here. But his motivation was noble, and that was all that mattered now.

He'd done it all for Kelly.

Before long, he would fulfill his aim, and then he'd have all the time in the world to consider the rights and wrongs of it all.

"So, what's the plan then?" Duncan, the self-styled leader of Ferris' troupe of warriors asked. The scars across his face told of a life lived by the sword. He wouldn't have given Ferris even one shred of respect, if it wasn't for the coin he'd been paid, and even then, he had a mind of his own.

Money could buy anything nowadays, especially a small army. Every single one of the men on board this ship had a few things in common: They were all battle-hardened, and they would do almost anything for the right price.

But that wasn't to say that they were easy to deal with.

"We must assume they guard their territory. Therefore, we'll hide in plain sight, pretending to be fishermen," Ferris said. "Once the rest of the ships get here, that's when we'll make our move."

"We look like fishermen to you?" one of the other mercenaries quipped, exposing a toothless grin.

A roar of laughter erupted among the rest of the group, who had so far just stood by in silence.

Ferris straightened himself. He wasn't going to let any one of these men ruin this moment. They hadn't seen the worst of him yet.

He closed his eyes and focused his energy.

For but a moment, the skies darkened above the ship, and the low rumble of thunder could be heard. Most of the fighters shuffled around uncomfortably.

Ferris calmed himself before speaking. Suspicions and rumor were all well and good, but magic was one of the few things these men did fear. If he took things too far, they'd bolt and there would be nobody left to fight alongside him.

"You'd better be convincing, or we'll fail before we

even get close enough. And guess what, failure won't get you paid," Ferris warned. "Hide your weapons and armor, then cast nets out into the water!"

"Alright," Duncan grumbled, and nodded at the rest of the group.

Some muttered words of protest, but eventually everyone fell in line. Again, these were men who would do nearly anything for money.

Ferris watched them in silence as they got to work.

He had a plan, of course, but he wasn't going to share it with any of them, even Duncan. Over the years he had discovered talents that went far beyond summoning a few clouds up in the sky.

He had learned to separate his mind and body. If he found a suitable vessel to transport into, a flying animal perhaps, he could travel great distances seemingly without having moved at all.

If this ship could get him near enough, he would easily be able to reach the Black Isles, at least in spirit.

All he needed was another life form within view, ideally a bird, for his spirit to latch onto.

While he and his animal host gathered information about the enemy, his body would remain where it was on this ship, waiting for his return. And then….

He rubbed his hands together. He could already picture it. King Harrold would claim the victory as his own, but that hardly mattered to Ferris. It wasn't glory he was after.

It wasn't even the riches he had promised his men.

Sweet revenge.

He would see the Isles reduced to mere ruins and take his sister home with him where she belonged. The giant warriors of Black Isle would not be allowed to tear apart another human family. He would make sure of it.

At the end of this fight, the treaty between the men of the mainland and the giants of Black Isle would end. The coming summer would mark a new era where no lottery would take place. No unsuspecting girl would be abandoned on the beaches of West Hythe, awaiting a fate worse than death as a human sacrifice to these barbarians.

Once the deck was cleared of any weaponry and other suspicious items, and the nets had been cast, Ferris retreated into his cabin and peered out of the porthole.

From there he would bide his time and wait for the right opportunity.

And sure enough, only a short while later, a small speck appeared on the horizon.

A bird.

Ferris squinted at it to get a better look. *Come closer!*

His spirit could not travel long distances from his body, so he still had to wait. Unfortunately, the animal did not approach the ship at all, but instead turned away.

Curious.

No matter, there were still many hours left in the day. Ferris was certain he'd get another chance. He had waited a long time to get here, what were a few hours more? The other ships weren't even within sight yet. He'd have plenty of time to infiltrate the Isles, locate Kelly, and get back, before anyone even found his empty body.

CHAPTER TWO

"Eryn! Mistress Eryn!" a frantic voice called out to her.

She looked up from the large leather-bound volume in front of her. There stood the same new recruit whom she had reprimanded before shift. His shoulder-length hair was in a mess and his eyes wide as they darted back and forth between her and the Elders also present in the library. His breathing was labored, as though he'd been running before he got here.

"Yes?" she asked.

"Silence in the library," one of Eryn's white-haired reading companions snapped.

The boy hadn't even had the chance to answer her yet.

She made a calming gesture with her hand and got up from her seat. Eryn guided the boy out of the library and into the corridor, where Yorrick just happened to be passing by.

The latter stopped in his tracks when he spotted the two eagles.

"What's happened?" she asked the boy again.

"There's a ship, a human ship I reckon," he said.

Yorrick turned to face Eryn with a questioning look on his face. She shook her head and gestured at him to keep quiet.

"A human ship, where?" Eryn asked.

The young eagle tried to explain the directions, out of breath as he was.

"What were they doing?" Yorrick jumped in.

Eryn shot him a look of disapproval. The boy was already so confused, the last thing he needed was to be interrogated by two superiors instead of just one.

"I dunno, I mean there were nets and things. Perhaps they're fishing. But you don't see humans around these waters, do you? I mean, I've never seen any on previous shifts."

Eryn nodded. He was as yet inexperienced. He'd never accompanied a hunting party to the mainland even. Perhaps it was just the shock of seeing people other than their own kind that had gotten him so riled up.

"Thank you for letting me know. I'll take it from here," Eryn said as she turned toward Yorrick.

"Do we attack them? What do we do?" the boy asked.

She turned back momentarily.

"I said, I'll take it from here. If they're just fishermen, there is no need to panic."

He did not look convinced.

Neither did Yorrick, who slowly shook his head at her.

Eryn waited for a moment, but the boy did not move from her side.

"That will be all," she added in a firmer tone.

The young eagle nodded and hesitated for a moment

before turning away. She had often wished for certain members of her squad to show more interest in their jobs, but right now she desired the opposite. This matter was not his concern.

"We need to call a Council meeting," Yorrick spoke under his breath.

"My thoughts exactly, but first I'm going to take a look for myself. Assess the threat."

Yorrick nodded.

"Don't be long. In the meantime, I'll get everyone assembled in the Great Hall," he said.

"Be careful."

"Of course." Eryn left him with a nod and raced to the View Point.

She leapt off the edge and closed her eyes as the wind started to carry her. She dove down the side of the castle wall to collect more speed, then straightened her path in the direction where the boy had supposedly seen the ship.

She was fast. It wouldn't take her long.

Indeed, she had only been flying for ten minutes or so when she saw the vessel bobbing in the waves ahead. The ship did not look typical for what she'd seen of human fishing boats during her excursions onto the mainland. But then again, the local villagers did not venture into these waters. They knew better.

Perhaps these were travelers from further away.

Nothing she saw down below alarmed her too much. The boy who first spotted them had clearly overreacted, inexperienced as he was.

She'd head back soon to report on this sighting, and get a couple of more senior members of her squad to keep an eye on things in the meantime. There seemed to be no immediate reason to panic. Planning an intervention didn't even occur to her.

Until….

The shock nearly threw Eryn out of the sky. Only thanks to her quick reflexes was she able to recover her trajectory. The pull on her from below was immense, and her thoughts became garbled for a moment. She was able to fight the strange sensation that had threatened to overcome her, but with great difficulty.

Something, or more precisely, someone was trying to affect Eryn.

Witchcraft.

Eryn was familiar with the feeling of having someone rummage around in your thoughts. Her training with Rhea had included several sessions with Queen Kelly, practicing her own magic on her.

This was something similar, and yet there were two very striking differences: She hadn't expected it and thus was unprepared. And this wasn't Queen Kelly, but a total stranger. A potential threat.

It was the violation more than anything that had panicked her so.

Helpless, vulnerable. No amount of combat training

could help her in the face of such sorcery.

Still, she managed to collect herself somewhat and focus on her duty.

Who are you? Eryn thought.

She circled the sky above the human ship once more and peered down.

The men at work appeared to be fishermen indeed. Half a dozen or so were pulling in a net onto the deck. Others were sitting around just watching the goings on while enjoying a leisurely smoke.

Humans or islanders, some things were not so different after all. A fair number of them seemed to not take their jobs too seriously.

None paid her any attention. Why would they? The only way for her to take flight was to fully transform, so they had no way of knowing she wasn't just an ordinary bird.

Still, she was missing something. These simple-looking men hadn't caused the bizarre sensation she'd felt only moments ago.

But as she circled around once more, she felt a surge of energy and immediately peered down at the source.

Witch!

If she hadn't been looking specifically for it, she would have never noticed the pair of steely blue eyes staring up at her from a small porthole below deck. There he was, her intruder. But what was he trying to achieve?

The longer she looked at him, the more uneasy she

became. Her heart raced ever faster. Every instinct she had told her to run and let someone else deal with the problem.

But she didn't. She kept on staring into those mysterious eyes locked onto hers, trying to read their intent. Hidden behind his beauty was an unmistakable darkness. He was on his own mission, just as she was.

Danger.

Anger welled up inside her. These were no ordinary fishermen after all. There was a reason these humans had ventured so far into their territory, bringing their witchcraft with them.

Remembering her duty to her people, Eryn broke eye contact with the strange man and raced straight toward Black Mountain. Broc, Rhea, the Elders, everyone had to be informed immediately. They needed to mobilize the army.

For the first time in many years, they would have to gear up for a fight.

———◆———

Ferris' earlier assumption had been correct. After the first bird's sudden departure, another appeared relatively quickly.

It was a type of eagle and rather large too. Brown with white accents on its wings. You saw them sometimes on the mainland, especially around the White Cliff, though this was a particularly majestic specimen. He focused his energy again and readied himself for his bodily departure.

Although he'd left his physical form behind, his mind wasn't getting anywhere. No matter how hard he tried, he could not enter the animal. He looked down at himself and saw he was somewhere halfway between the ship and where he'd first seen the animal.

The eagle, meanwhile, had circled around the ship and came into view once more, then paused in his line of sight. It hovered high above the surface of the water, as though it was looking for something.

Ferris withdrew into his body again and realized what was going on. The eagle was staring down right into his eyes. A shiver traveled down the back of his neck.

How ridiculous. It was just an animal, after all.

Ferris shook off his unease and tried again as hard he could, this time with his eyes closed for extra focus. Usually the transition happened so quickly, he'd slip into his target within a split second. But not today.

His heart started pounding and the veins on the side of his head began to throb. The exertion was immense, and yet he was getting nowhere. Any more and his head might explode.

He exhaled and opened his eyes just in time to see the bird turn away and make a quick escape. It looked like it was fleeing something. As if it had noticed the attempted intrusion and become spooked.

Again, that was ridiculous.

Ferris looked down, trying to catch his breath. His knuckles had turned white; that was how hard he'd been holding on to the ledge of his cabin window.

He'd mastered this talent years ago, so why had he been unable to take over the eagle's body this time? This had never happened to him before.

He couldn't recall the last time he'd messed up a bodily departure. Sure, in the beginning he'd had trouble focusing. He'd sometimes ended up in the wrong animal, especially when practicing on a group of them at once. Birds in particular were one of the easier species, not like dogs or cats, which were much harder to control.

Still, he'd never been entirely unsuccessful. *Except....*

After mastering his skills on various birds and other creatures, he'd once attempted to take over a human body. The resistance he'd felt was immense. It had nearly knocked him out, as well as the villager on whom he had tried his magic. Afterwards, he was fatigued for days.

And so he had never attempted it again.

This failure reminded him of that old experiment gone wrong.

Ferris took a step back and sat down on his cot. It couldn't be, surely. Unless someone else, another warlock, had already transported themselves into that eagle.

Could it be that he was not alone? That there were others out there who possessed similar powers, perhaps on the Black Isles themselves?

For so long he'd assumed he was the only one of his kind. But it *was* possible that others possessed similar powers, wasn't it?

And if this assumption was correct, he had much more to worry about. The animal had turned around rather abruptly. Ferris had to assume that he wasn't the only one who felt something was off.

If another warlock had occupied that bird, he had to consider that his presence in these waters was no longer a secret. As convincing as their fishermen act had been, now the game was up.

The element of surprise he had banked on to make their incursion a success was gone.

Ferris startled into action and hurried onto the upper deck.

"Gather your weapons and gear up!" he shouted. "We are about to be discovered!"

As he watched his men jump into action and gather their swords and armor, Ferris could only hope for two things.

That King Harrold had kept his promise, and secondly, that his navy would reach these waters in time for the first battle.

CHAPTER THREE

E ryn burst through the doors of the Great Hall and found the Council already assembled, ready for the meeting to begin. Yorrick had kept his word.

"My King, we have a big problem," Eryn blurted out.

Broc, King of the Black Isles, waited in silence, while the Elders and Yorrick were engaged in hushed conversation.

Rhea rushed ahead and took Eryn aside.

"I wish you'd informed me before storming in here like this," she whispered.

Eryn averted her gaze. "I apologize, General Rhea, but there is no time to waste. We are under threat."

Yorrick looked up from his discussion and joined the two women.

"All this unfolded moments before I called the meeting," he said.

Rhea let her gaze pause on Yorrick for a moment, but then turned back to Eryn and gave her a nod. She was not pleased; the tense expression on her face made that very clear. Perhaps this was in part because Yorrick had been involved from the start, whereas she had so far been unaware.

But whether or not Rhea was happy about it did not matter. This *was* an emergency.

"Very well then," Rhea spoke more loudly this time. "Please tell us your findings."

Eryn cleared her throat.

"I don't know what, if anything, Yorrick has told you already. This morning one of my squad of lookouts spotted what appeared to be a human fishing boat in our waters."

"Well, that's something new," Saras, Rhea's mate spoke up.

Eryn frowned at him. This wasn't something to be smiling about. And what was he doing in this meeting? Saras was not a member of the Council as far as she knew.

"If only it were a fishing boat. Things are not how they appear. There's a witch on board. He tried to infiltrate my mind as I was circling the vessel to gather information about them, but I think I managed to fight him off, so he wouldn't have learned anything of value from me."

"A male witch is called a warlock, dear," Saras interrupted. He was still smiling, and Eryn was getting more and more annoyed with his casual attitude.

"Thank you, Saras. A warlock, then," Eryn snapped.

Just how Rhea could stand the dragon, she did not know. Love clearly made you stupid.

Broc stepped up and raised his hands. "This is no time for petty arguments. We need to take this seriously. A human vessel with a warlock on board is trying to get close to our territory. This has to be interpreted as a threat against us, and we should take action. Rhea?"

Finally, someone who understood the gravity of the situation.

Rhea gave Eryn a disapproving look. She hated to be out of the loop on this one. Again, Eryn did not let it bother her. She had done what she thought was right for the good of their people.

"My King, I think we should take action immediately," Rhea said. "I'll send a group of our best fighters out to capture the ship and all its occupants. We'll sort out if they're fishermen or not, once they're safely tucked away in our dungeons."

Eryn nodded. This was the best course of action, she had to agree.

"Anything to add, Uri?" Broc turned to face the leader of the Elders. "A prophecy to fit, perhaps?"

Uri turned a darker shade of red. "My King, I have nothing of that sort to report. But of course we'll study the matter as soon as this meeting is over."

Eryn looked around the room. Everyone, except for Saras, appeared to be taking the matter seriously. But there was someone missing in today's meeting, the one person whose input she would have loved to hear the most.

"Where's our Queen today?" Eryn asked.

Rhea shot her another disapproving look.

Broc turned to face her and folded his arms in front of his chest. "The queen's presence is not compulsory at every one of these meetings."

"Obviously not, my King, it's just that she is the only one on this island with firsthand experience of magic," Eryn spoke in a more apologetic tone. "It would have been good to get her input on this."

"I will inform her accordingly," Broc said. "But I think Rhea's men can manage to deal with a handful of fishermen and a rather untalented mind reader, without disturbing the queen at this time."

Eryn bit her lip and nodded, though she disagreed. She'd been able to resist the warlock's influence so far, but who knew what other magic he was capable of. Perhaps they ought to minimize the risk altogether. Perhaps….

"That will be all then. Rhea, I want your best men on board our fastest ship at the earliest. Capture the humans alive, if you can. And don't transform unless it's absolutely inevitable. Best we don't reveal all our secrets just yet."

Rhea nodded and turned on her heel, heading for the door. Eryn did her best to keep up.

"I really wish I'd known about this," Rhea grumbled as the two women marched through the hallway leading towards the armory.

"There wasn't any time."

"And what is it with Yorrick turning up everywhere, getting involved?" Rhea complained. "You steer clear of him, you hear me? It's obvious what he's trying to do."

"Oh?" Eryn frowned.

"He's trying to recruit you to the Castle Guard. It's so obvious. But I need your full attention on our work here.

We've had a good few years of peace, but it looks like those days are behind us now."

Eryn did not respond, just kept on walking half a step behind Rhea.

Just as they arrived in front of the armory, Rhea paused and turned around.

"Eryn, do you trust me?" she asked.

Eryn swallowed hard. "Yes. Yes, of course, General Rhea."

"Our King has given his orders, but I could tell you weren't satisfied."

Eryn pressed her lips together. Where was Rhea going with this?

"I'm going to send you along on this mission. But I want you to do something for me. Promise you won't speak a word of it to anyone."

"Anything you need, my General," Eryn's voice had turned into a whisper.

"You'll focus solely on the warlock. If you think he's a bigger threat than Broc assumes, you'll eliminate him, you hear me?"

Eryn was stunned to silence for a moment. Sure, she had thought the same during the Council Meeting. But to hear Rhea say it out loud….

"We can't risk bringing him onto Black Mountain," Eryn mumbled.

Rhea reached for Eryn's arm and gave it a squeeze. "So,

I can trust you with this?"

Eryn nodded. "You have my word."

"Right. Let's do this." Rhea turned and opened the armory door.

Inside, a handful of soldiers had already gathered for their afternoon shift. Poor bastards. Little did they know that today wasn't the quiet day they had been looking forward to.

Eryn took a deep breath as she followed Rhea inside.

"Guys, we have a development," Rhea started. "Moments earlier a human ship has been spotted in our waters. They appear to be fishermen, but that could be an act. We have orders to capture them."

Everyone present perked up immediately upon Rhea's announcement. There was not a whisper to be heard.

Eryn, meanwhile, shuffled restlessly from one foot to the other.

Rhea glanced at her for a moment, then focused once more on her men.

"We must assume they're a threat," Rhea said. "You'll go in fully geared up and ready for anything. But in *human* form, alright? Do not reveal your true nature!"

Eryn continued to hold her breath. Rhea had confided in her, but she hadn't told these soldiers what awaited them on that ship.

Rhea turned to face Eryn, her eyes softening slightly. "Eryn will be in charge of the humans' capture. These are your King's orders; capture them alive unless there's no other way. I'll be waiting here for your return."

"Let's go get us some humans," one of the more experienced soldiers spoke with glee.

"Remember, we want them alive," Rhea urged, then let her gaze settle on Eryn's before continuing. "Unless there's no other way."

Eryn nodded slowly. She couldn't fault Rhea's orders. They needed the humans alive, to figure out if more trouble was brewing. But the warlock…. He was a liability no matter what.

Still, the thought of what she had to do weighed heavily on Eryn's conscience. Sure, she was well trained and confident of her combat skills.

But she'd never taken a life before.

All Eryn could hope for was that the warlock would put up a fight and provoke her. In the heat of the moment, instinct took over. Only then would she not hesitate to do what had to be done.

—◆—

Ferris stood at the helm of his ship once more.

But it wasn't an easy victory he was anticipating this time. If his predictions were correct, he had led them right into a trap. And their backup was nowhere within view yet.

"Up ahead!" one of his fighters shouted as they pointed at something in the distance.

Ferris followed his line of sight and indeed spotted something on the horizon. It was hard to make out against the dark backdrop of the rocky Isles, but the closer it came, the more obvious it was.

An enemy ship. Sails flapped in the firm gusts battering this inhospitable sea.

Ferris breathed in deeply and tightened his grip on the butt of his sword until his knuckles showed white.

He'd proved himself a skilled fighter over the years, but would he be good enough when pitched against the giants? He would soon find out. Of course, he still had his hidden talents to help him if all else failed.

"Your orders?" Duncan's gruff voice interrupted his thoughts.

Ferris glanced at the man. "You're not scared, are you?"

Duncan scoffed and spat on the deck. "You forget, this isn't my first battle. If you're not sure how to handle it, I'll take over command."

How to handle it?

Duncan was right, Ferris had to step up be a leader now. It wasn't just their life at stake here, it was Kelly's as well. Her safety trumped everything. And he would be no good to her if he perished so early in the game.

"The royal navy cannot be far behind us. Best we save our strength for the next battle. You'll put up enough of a fight as to not make them suspicious, but our aim is to buy time," Ferris said.

Duncan frowned. "You mean for us to let ourselves be

captured?"

"If it comes to that. By all means, if you're capable of an easy victory, go for it. But it's early days yet in this war. Don't fight to the death. We must live to win another day."

"They catch us, we'll be dead anyway!" another fighter complained. "I heard the giants eat children for breakfast!"

"You're not a child, are you?" Ferris snapped. "You're fighters, all of you. Survivors! If we make sure they don't kill us on the spot, they'll want to keep us and question us. That's what I would do if I found a foreign ship within my borders."

Duncan and Ferris shared a long, silent stare. In the end, the mercenary looked away to address his men. Ferris had won this leadership challenge at least.

"You heard the man," Duncan said. "Fight, but let them win without too much bloodshed. We'll be resting on the Black Isles tonight."

"Once the King's ships get here, we'll take advantage of the confusion and make our escape," Ferris added. "We'll attack them from the inside. We'll outnumber them! Our victory is inevitable!"

A reluctant whisper traveled the crowd. Most of the fighters looked skeptical. Still, nobody had the balls to argue aloud, neither with Ferris nor with Duncan.

"Your sacrifice will be handsomely rewarded!" Ferris said.

The promise of money generally worked. Today was no

different.

Most of the men visibly perked up and their earlier complaints were drowned out by the clanging of armor and weapons as they started to spread around the deck.

"Take cover, they might have archers," Duncan added.

Sure enough, by the time every last one of them had found a suitable hiding place, the first couple of arrows started to fly past. Warning shots.

Ferris tried to control his emotions and keep his mind clear. Accidentally summoning a thunderstorm would only draw unnecessary attention to himself. If an enemy warlock was indeed out there somewhere, he'd be wise not to expose himself too soon.

As the enemy ship stopped alongside his starboard side, he emerged from his cover, sword held high, and charged forward. He was determined put up a good show, just as he had ordered his soldiers-for-hire to do.

And he would have, if only the first enemy fighter to jump on board hadn't distracted him so.

CHAPTER FOUR

It was unmistakably him. Eryn was instantly mesmerized by the man's eyes.

This was the one who had attempted to read her mind as she had flown past the ship earlier, staring up at her from his cabin, assuming she wouldn't notice.

Only, she *had* noticed.

Now here he stood, his sword held high, circling her in a bid to evade the aim of her bow and arrow. He wouldn't be able to, of course. She was faster than any human. More accurate.

And she had orders to kill. All it took was one swift flick of her finger. The arrow would hit any body part of her choosing instantly.

Time seemed to stand still for her, as soldiers rushed past and clashed with the other humans. The latter were no match, of course. Every single one of her fighters had at least a foot or two on the feeble humans. But *her* opponent was different.

The warlock was unique.

He stood taller than his companions, with broad, muscular shoulders to match. They were about equally matched as far as height went. And he looked younger than the others, probably closer to her own age.

His blue eyes hid all sorts of sins.

But these superficial observations hadn't shaken Eryn. As physically impressive as he was for one of his breed, Eryn had been affected by a much deeper power.

It must be his magic, she thought. And yet she felt no sign of his presence in her own mind.

Strange.

All she could do was observe him, as though she was not truly in control of her body.

Then, the spell was broken by his first move. He charged ahead and swung at her with his sword, and instantly she snapped out of her trance.

She defended herself with her bow, whipping it around to break the impact of his weapon, then swiftly flung it over her shoulder and unsheathed a blade of her own.

They danced around each other, eyes locked on, taking turns to attack and defend. But his impact lacked strength. Were humans really that much weaker? Or was he as reluctant as she was to do real damage?

Where had her hesitation come from? She didn't have time for this!

Eryn bit her bottom lip as she swung around again. In this carefully orchestrated charade of a fight, it was her turn to strike. She'd had enough of the pretense and more importantly, she had orders to follow.

She raised her sword and aimed. He stepped aside to evade her attack, just as she suspected he'd do. In response, she changed direction mid-swing, found an opening, and brought the tip of her blade to a halt right at his throat.

It would be so easy to push a little harder and draw blood. So easy, and yet impossibly difficult. With a heavy heart she realized she couldn't finish it. She couldn't bring herself to kill him.

"You'd better drop that sword," she hissed.

The man did as he was told, but his expression was as calm as it had been all along. Like this wasn't a real fight, and he hadn't really been defeated.

"I surrender." As he spoke, the corner of his mouth curled up just slightly.

Was he smiling?

Eryn could not be sure. All she knew was that the longer she looked at his boyishly handsome face, the deeper she would sink. He'd given up so quickly, she couldn't even justify carrying out Rhea's demand here. Not in full view of her soldiers, who had been given clear orders to keep the prisoners alive.

So in a way, it was she who had lost this fight after all.

Rhea would be furious and rightly so. She was angry with herself.

A quick glance around revealed that most of the other humans had surrendered as well. If this was the sum total of the threat against the Isles, then they had nothing to worry about. As she looked back at her own prisoner, something shook Eryn to her core. His expression was so relaxed, it almost looked smug. There was something more coming.

She might regret capturing him alive before the day was over.

"Tie them up and stash them below deck, then we'll tow the entire ship back to Black Mountain," Eryn ordered. "Good fight, everyone!"

Her soldiers let out a loud cheer before getting to work and doing what she'd ordered. Eryn stood back and let someone else secure the ropes around the warlock's wrists.

There was something about him that she could not understand. She wasn't just apprehensive of his powers; it wasn't fear she felt.

Yet she dare not touch him. Or look him in the eye for too long.

Her heart was beating just a little too fast. Her breaths had become too shallow. If she didn't know any better, she thought it might be nerves. A funny tickle in the depths of her stomach made it hard for her to remain focused.

If she was in fact nervous, there was another, heavier feeling making things worse. A deep sadness had crept into her chest. It tore at her, and dragged her down.

It was only once he was completely out of sight that she could breathe a little more freely.

———◆———

Back on shore, everyone had a job to do. Every one of her fighters had one or two prisoners of their own to attend to, so Eryn couldn't palm the warlock off on anyone else.

She was stuck with him.

That same sick feeling she'd felt earlier on the human ship had crept over her again.

She kept him walking just slightly ahead of her, all the while scanning her surroundings. It had taken them a while to travel back to the harbor with the enemy ship in tow. The barren, windswept landscape looked almost ominous in the fading daylight.

It wasn't just his sight that had her confused. Even the scent of him had an effect on her. Like a kind of musk, it tried to conjure up feelings she had no use for. Eryn tried to keep her breaths shallow to avoid the worst of it.

Was this what failure felt like? She'd never disappointed Rhea before....

As much as she dreaded facing the General's judgment, it was nothing compared to the prospect of making eye contact with her prisoner again.

The journey up to Black Mountain from the harbor below felt a thousand times as long. Thankfully, he hadn't uttered a word since his capture. Not like the other prisoners, who had cursed and spat at their captors.

"Lower the Drawbridge. Prisoners coming through," she ordered in a firm voice. If only she felt as confident as she sounded.

The bridge shuddered and creaked into action. A dozen pairs of eyes were upon them.

She felt a thin layer of sweat collect on her brow.

Let them not notice!

As Rhea's right-hand woman, she couldn't afford a humiliation like this. *Do not show weakness in front of the outsider!*

Once inside, they were surrounded by guards. The familiar smells of home mingled with the invasive scent of the warlock. But that did nothing to lessen its effect, instead it made it worse.

Eryn and the others marched the prisoners down the cold stone steps into the dungeon. There were few cells, so they had to accommodate multiple humans in each one. But she'd lock up her prisoner alone in the farthest, darkest corner. Not that these precautions would help settle her nerves.

Earlier today, he'd tried to invade her mind. Now he had invaded her home.

She watched as the guards locked up. A number of rusty metal doors creaked in place, each secured with heavy bolts and padlocks.

Eryn turned on her heel and started to walk away. It took all the self-discipline she could muster not to break into a run, or better yet, simply fly off as fast as she could.

And still, with each passing step, she did not feel relief as expected. Instead, the burden of his presence weighed on her heavier as the distance between them grew.

Like a shroud of sadness, taking away the last spot of light in her heart.

No matter what happened with Rhea now, she knew she wouldn't find rest tonight. Not with *him* down here.

The confidence she'd felt only this morning had been wiped away. In its place, a crushing sense of doom.

She ought to extinguish it. Kill him, where he stood. The guards wouldn't even notice if she did it right; not until it was too late. But not without talking to Rhea first.

———◆———

S o that was interesting. Interesting, and completely inexplicable.

Not only had Ferris allowed himself to be captured by a woman—and what a woman she was—there was something familiar about her. The look in her eyes suggested she'd recognized him too.

But for all his certainty, he could not place her at all. He'd traveled extensively over the years, but she was from the Black Isles. A so-called giant, though she wasn't any taller than he was. Still, she was formidable for a woman.

And her physique was unlike anything he'd seen before. Not like the girls he'd grown up with. Raw muscle, without any hint of softness or femininity that he could see.

Her lack of vulnerability did not make her any less appealing, though. Quite the opposite.

She had locked him up all alone, without any of his men for company. He couldn't fault her for that. He would have done the same thing in her shoes. The last thing his captors needed was for him to orchestrate a revolt down here.

The cell was cold, inhospitable, and utterly dark. They'd taken everyone underground, so there were no windows. The air smelled musty and damp. Probably this place hadn't been in regular use.

His current situation complicated his escape plans. If only there was some animal around for him to take over. He'd at least be able to start looking for Kelly….

Still, there were upsides to being imprisoned alone. He would hear no complaints from his men. Ferris had only his own thoughts to keep himself company.

And by God, he had a lot to think about.

During their capture, he hadn't seen any sign of magic. The islanders hadn't needed it; with their superior strength and imposing physiques, they would have defeated his men with ease, even if they hadn't surrendered.

But there had to be another warlock around these lands somewhere. It was the only thing that could explain his baffling experience with the eagle.

And then there was the woman… She alone could occupy his thoughts for the rest of his natural life.

Ferris explored his cell by touch, running his hands along the smooth, cold walls. It wasn't very large; it didn't take him long to feel his way along the irregular shaped walls back to the rough metal door.

Locked . Of course it was.

The only hope of getting out of here was if someone opened it from the outside.

Ferris felt his way to the deepest part of his cell and lowered himself onto the ground. There was a rough cloth-like item on the ground, probably a jute sack of some sort. He sat on top of it and rested his back against the wall.

The cold started to creep into his skin. His fingertips and toes already started to numb. There was no point in fighting it. He'd conserve his energy and wait.

Until someone or something got him out of here.

CHAPTER FIVE

"I thought I could trust you to do the right thing," Rhea hissed.

Eryn kept her eyes fixed on the ground between the two of them. She'd messed up, and she knew it.

"He just surrendered. What was I going to do? Slit his throat in plain view of all the other soldiers?"

Rhea paced the room, as she often did when she was upset.

"Perhaps that would have been better than the mess we're in now. Now he's *here*, in our very home!"

Eryn sighed and shook her head. Rhea was right, of course. Nothing she said was anything Eryn hadn't already thought about. "It's not ideal. I also would have preferred if we hadn't brought him here. But the King's orders—"

"As you know I have great respect for our King, but in this instance, he's wrong. We mustn't underestimate the warlock's powers. We mustn't allow ourselves to become easy targets."

"Right." Eryn shuffled from one foot to the other.

"And the longer we leave him in the dungeon, the more chances he'll get to outwit us with his magic. So tonight, after the feast is over, you'll finish it. When I wake up in the morning, I want some good news."

"You mean…." Eryn bit her lip.

"Do I have to spell it out? You'll go down there at night. The guards will have had their fill of food and wine by then, so they'll have inevitably fallen asleep. And you kill him."

Eryn nodded and closed her eyes. It was the right call. To finish what she had been unable to on the ship earlier. "Yes, General Rhea."

Just how she was meant to fulfill Rhea's demands without drawing suspicions on herself, she had no idea.

"Good. Our fate lies quite literally in your hands."

"I won't let you down," Eryn whispered, even if she already had her doubts.

If she was entirely honest with herself, she knew that she could have killed him during their fight. But she hadn't the will, or perhaps even the courage.

Possibly he'd put a spell on her. And if that was the case, then nothing would stop him from doing it again tonight.

Still, Rhea wasn't in the mood for arguments, so Eryn kept her doubts to herself. With a bit of hope, the prisoner would be asleep and it would all be over soon.

She excused herself and made her way along the endless corridors of the castle towards the Great Hall, where many of the men had already assembled.

King Broc had arranged a hearty meal for all his fighters and everyone in the castle was invited. They were to celebrate the successful capture of the enemy ship.

Wine and ale were flowing freely already. Morale was at an all-time high.

However, Eryn had nothing much to feel joyous about. All she could think about was the warlock, and what she had to do come nightfall.

The more she mulled it over, the sadder she felt. Either about the idea of killing him, or the possibility that she'd fail again.

Ferris had no idea how long he'd been locked up. He'd drifted in and out of sleep multiple times. Without any connection to the outside world, it was impossible to judge how much time had passed.

His eyes could not adjust to the darkness, so he didn't even know what his cell really looked like. All he knew was that he was alone.

Or he had been until a moment ago.

Ferris breathed in deeply, letting his other senses take over where his sight was failing him.

She was here. Her scent clung to the cold, damp air. Floral and fresh, like a flowering meadow in early summer.

He opened his eyes, still saw only darkness.

Should he say something? But what?

What could she possibly want?

Presumably he was about to find out.

A soft breath tickled his face, as ice cold steel pressed up against his throat.

There it was. She had come for his life.

He didn't fear death, he simply regretted having failed Kelly. Still, there was a certain comfort in knowing how it all would end.

He waited with bated breath, but nothing happened. The blade started to warm up against his skin. Her shallow breaths continued to brush against his cheek.

It was a bittersweet sensation, feeling her presence so close. It hardly mattered if her aim was to end him, or perhaps that made it even sweeter.

Was that why she was dragging things out? Had she sensed his attraction and did she feel the same way?

Or was she waiting for his last words, perhaps? Maybe he was dreaming the whole thing.

"What...." Ferris' voice cracked. His throat had become dry. "What's the meaning of this?"

The pressure on the blade reduced, and suddenly, she lifted it off his throat.

"I have orders to kill you," the woman whispered.

Ferris nodded. "I understand. I deserve as much."

They were mortal enemies. He ought to want to kill her too, though he didn't, not really.

"But...."

"But?" he asked, then smiled briefly when he realized what she was trying to say. "You can't do it."

There was a soft shuffle nearby, as though the woman had sat down on the ground beside him.

"I can't do it," she said.

Although he hadn't been afraid to die, it was still a relief to hear her say that. He might complete his mission here yet. Had he found an unexpected ally in this woman, who had come to kill him and failed?

"That's awkward," he said.

"How so?" she asked.

"Well, it will be when you have to face whoever gave you the order."

"Right. Awkward." The woman sighed.

Encouraged by their unusual interaction so far, Ferris decided to ask her just what had been on his mind all along.

"Tell me, where have I seen you before?"

"What makes you think you have?" she asked.

Ferris smiled and shook his head. Of course she didn't make it easy. They never did. But he had to unravel this mystery, one way or another.

"I saw the way you looked at me. There was recognition in your eyes," he said.

Muffled voices on the other side of his cell door interrupted their conversation.

"Why is this unlocked?" another female voice spoke. "Open it! Show me who's in there!"

"Shit," his female companion cursed under her breath, then shuffled away from him.

The door creaked open, letting in a dim ray of light which finally allowed Ferris to see the inside of his cell. There was nothing much to see. A dirty stone floor, the jute sack he'd been sitting on all this time, and solid walls made out of hewn granite.

There was no sign of the woman who'd kept him company so far, then again, the shadowy corner beside the door was still obscured in darkness.

But as soon as his new visitor appeared, Ferris forgot all about that, and rushed onto his feet.

"Kelly!" His voice cracked again as he called out to his sister.

The past six or so years had changed her. It wasn't just the strange clothes she was wearing, or the way she now kept her hair. He'd remembered her as a girl, and now she was unmistakably a woman. Still, he'd know her anywhere.

She was the motivation for everything he had done all these years. His sole reason for coming here.

"Oh, Ferris!" Kelly rushed toward him and threw her arms around his neck.

Ferris wrapped his arms tightly around Kelly's shoulders. To be reunited, after such a long time.

Had he lost his mind? Had all the events in his cell so far been part of an elaborate hallucination? Perhaps it was the enemy warlock, trying to break him. First with an attractive woman, now with a vision of his sister.

But it felt so real. If this was just an illusion, he couldn't resist its charm. Even her scent was as he remembered. As he buried his nose in Kelly's hair, he felt as though he'd come home.

"When they said they'd captured some mainlanders, I had no idea…. If I had known it was you, I would have come down here sooner!" Kelly said.

Tears were streaming down her face.

Ferris was overwhelmed by his own emotions. He'd dreamed about it for so long, about how their reunion would go. Never once did he consider a scenario quite like this.

It didn't matter, though. All that mattered was that they were together again.

"Ever since I found out you'd been picked in the lottery…. I've been working to get you back. But what was I going to do? I was a scrawny seventeen-year old with no combat skills. I'm so sorry I couldn't come look for you sooner!"

Kelly pulled back and looked at him with a smile on her face. "It's quite alright. I've been well taken care of here."

Ferris frowned. Was this the aim of the deception? To convince him she was happy here?

"What are you talking about? You were taken against your will, and made to live on this barren rock in the sea," he said.

Kelly let out a chuckle. "Yes, that's what it seemed like at the start, but really, it's not so bad. I'll have you know,

I'm queen, now!"

Ferris opened his mouth in protest, but didn't get any words out. He stepped aside and peered at the as yet open door of his cell. A giant—roughly seven feet tall—stood guard. His impressive figure was somewhat marred by the sheepish expression on his face.

"Is that right?" Ferris wondered aloud.

"It's true. She's our queen," the guard mumbled, then turned away again and suppressed a yawn.

Just how this particular brand of magic worked, Ferris did not know. But assuming it was an illusion somehow made more sense than considering the alternative. That everything Kelly had told him so far was the truth.

———◆———

Eryn had listened in utter shock.

She never expected anyone to disturb her as she carried out Rhea's orders. The guards had all been asleep at their posts, just as predicted. Nobody had stirred even as Eryn unlocked the creaky door to the warlock's cell.

She'd waited for her eagle eyes to adjust to the darkness inside, and approached him directly with her weapon drawn. But at the last moment she faltered.

Another failure. Messing up was starting to become a habit of hers.

But to be caught unawares by the Queen, of all people?

Eryn did not know how to feel about it all. Brother and sister. Two humans with magical powers, reunited on Black Mountain. That was a big coincidence, now that she thought about it. It actually made sense.

In hindsight, her failure was for the best. She would have been caught standing over his body, the Queen's brother's blood on her hands. Rhea's anger would pale in comparison to Kelly's, as well as Broc's wrath.

Perhaps her instincts had tried to tell her something when she faltered. Perhaps her subconscious had known somehow that he was off limits to her blade.

Eryn held her breath and silently slid her weapon back into its sheath. It was easy to slip past the two humans; they could barely see in this light anyway.

The guard, meanwhile was too busy rubbing the last remnants of sleep and booze out of his eyes, so he was easy to get by as well.

But coming up the narrow corridor leading to the other prisoners, there was yet another unexpected sight for Eryn to contend with.

"My King," she said, and averted her gaze as she hurried past him. A handful of frazzled guards waited further up the corridor. Their awakening had been rude, no doubt.

"What's the meaning of all this? Wait a moment, Eryn, you're not going anywhere!"

"Yes, my King," Eryn mumbled and stopped in her tracks.

She slowly turned around to face King Broc, but avoided direct eye contact with him.

"First, I find my dungeons unguarded, on the one night when they are fully occupied with enemy fighters. And then I find you sneaking around these corridors? What business did you have down here?"

Eryn bit her lip. She had to come up with something, quickly.

"General Rhea…. She thought the prisoners might have some insights to share," Eryn whispered.

"What's that? You came down here reeking of ale, in an effort to interrogate these men? At this hour?"

"I…. I'm only following orders," Eryn said. It sounded more pathetic now that she'd said it aloud, even if it was technically true.

That Rhea had ordered her to kill the prisoner, rather than interrogate him, was only a minor twist of the truth.

"Broc!" another voice called out.

"Now what in the world?" Broc said. "Kelly, what are *you* doing here, in your condition?"

Eryn's heart was hammering in her throat now.

"Stop bothering Eryn, dear. She was only here to accompany me. You'll never guess who I found!"

"There's someone *else* here?" Broc exclaimed. "Next you'll tell me the entire council of Elders has decided to spend the night in the dungeons as well!"

Kelly smiled brightly, then nodded at Eryn. "You're

excused."

"Thank you, my Queen," Eryn mumbled. She breathed a sigh of relief as she rushed away, leaving the royal couple alone. This discussion was one they needed to have in private. Although grateful that the queen had covered for her, Eryn wanted no part of whatever came next.

Instead, she rushed straight up to Rhea's quarters to give her the latest.

CHAPTER SIX

erris couldn't believe what he had learned, even upon coming face to face with the man Kelly introduced as her husband of six years.

Broc Bearclaw, King of the Black Isles.

He could do little else but shake his head in disbelief.

And looking at the man, if you could call him that, it seemed he was as skeptical as Ferris himself.

"This is grand, isn't it? Reunited after all these years," Kelly said.

"Yes, it's wonderful," Ferris said, but his tone couldn't quite match her excitement.

"I can't wait for you to meet little Finlay," Kelly chatted on. "I'm sure he'll be thrilled to meet his human uncle."

"Wait, what?" Ferris and Broc spoke almost in unison.

"I don't think it would be wise bringing Finlay down here," Broc added.

Kelly shot him a disapproving look. "You're not seriously suggesting we leave my brother to rot in the dungeons?"

Ferris opened his mouth, then closed it again when he realized he had nothing useful to add.

"A strange and powerful magic," he mumbled to himself.

Broc turned to face him now, his arms folded across

his chest. "Indeed, let's talk about magic. So, you're a warlock, are you?"

Ferris met his stern gaze, which despite the giant's intentions did nothing to intimidate him. Since the topic was already broached, he'd better try to find out what he could. "I gather you have one of your own? A warlock, I mean?"

"What makes you think that?" Broc retorted.

The two men stared at each other in silence for a moment, their expressions as neutral as could be.

"Not a warlock, per se," Kelly interrupted.

Ferris cocked his head to the side and frowned. "*You?*"

She smiled knowingly. "I found out shortly after I reached here. Not too far from this cell, actually. It's a long story."

Broc cleared his throat. "I'm not sure this is the right time and place for this particular conversation."

"You're probably right," Kelly sighed, and placed her right hand on her lower abdomen. "In fact, why don't we retreat to more comfortable quarters?"

Broc stepped forward and placed his hand protectively on Kelly's shoulder. "Are you alright? Getting tired?"

She smiled up at him as they shared a look which made Ferris feel awkwardly out of place. Which, of course, he was. A third wheel, an unnecessary rescuer, invading what seemed to be a marriage unlike any he'd ever seen on the mainland.

He'd been wary of all he'd found here, and with good

reason. But the revelation that Kelly also possessed magical powers had soothed his suspicions somewhat. They were of the same blood. It made sense.

And she'd have no reason to deceive him.

"I'm fine," Kelly said. "But let's get my brother settled in a slightly better room now. We have much to catch up on."

Perhaps she really *was* happy here. Queen of the Black Isles, mother to a royal heir. With a husband who might look like a scary brute, but seemed to truly care for her wellbeing.

Ferris' mind was already spinning with all he had learned, when a sudden realization nearly made his heart stop. The royal navy…. it was still on its way!

"There's something you should know." Ferris briefly glanced at Broc, then settled his gaze on Kelly instead.

"Yes?"

"I had no way of knowing before speaking to you, but I'm afraid I've made a huge mistake," Ferris said. If all he had seen here was correct, even that was an understatement.

"Just what are you saying?" Broc interjected.

"We surrendered easily, let ourselves get captured by your men," Ferris began. "Because this was just the beginning. King Harrold of the mainland has sent a whole fleet of ships. Once they arrive in these waters, that's when the fight for the Black Isles will truly begin."

"Oh no," Kelly mumbled. "How many men are we talking about?"

Broc's face turned a few shades darker, and his eyes narrowed. "An invasion. How far out?"

That's where Ferris' answers ran out. "I cannot be sure how far out. We saw no sign of them when your ship found us. And I don't have exact numbers, but he assured me before I set off that he'd send sufficient troops. Perhaps a thousand. The villagers of the mainland are sick of the lottery. They don't want to send anymore daughters off to their deaths."

Realizing what he'd just said, Ferris quickly corrected himself. "I mean, in their minds, that's what happens. Although the reality seems slightly more complex, looking at Kelly's position here. The point is, they want out of the treaty, and they'll fight tooth and nail to get their way."

"We must wake the Council," Kelly stammered.

Broc did not say a word, though his eyes spoke a thousand words, none of them kind or gentle.

Ferris was overcome with regret. He had no way of knowing what he would find here. Naturally he'd assumed the worst. In informing them, at least Broc could prepare his men, but things would get ugly, as they always did in war.

Just how many lives Ferris' mistake would claim, he could not predict.

"What if I try to call things off?" Ferris wondered aloud. "If you release my men and me, and we return to the mainland and convince the King that an invasion is no longer necessary? Or perhaps I'll tell him he'll never win?"

"Do you think he'll be so easily convinced?" Kelly asked.

Broc shook his head. "No king worth his salt would give up so easily. He did not send out his navy on your word. He is doing it because he sees a chance at victory. And winning a battle against us will be worth more to him than your assurances, one way or another."

Ferris pressed his lips together. He hadn't made up his mind about whether he liked Broc yet. But he had to agree with his assessment.

"Let's talk to the Elders," Kelly said. "Perhaps they can come up with something better. Something that will actually help us."

Judging from his expression, Broc didn't like her suggestion either, but he chose not to argue. Most men Ferris knew wouldn't think twice about putting their wives in their place, no matter who was listening.

"At the very least we have to involve Rhea," Kelly urged.

"I'll call a Council meeting right now," Broc agreed.

Ferris stood by as Broc all but left the cell.

Kelly cleared her throat. "Darling, aren't you forgetting something?"

Broc stopped in his tracks and turned around slowly to study Ferris for a few silent moments.

"Very well…." Broc grumbled. "Guards!"

The same giant from before peeked inside again. "Yes, my King?"

"This prisoner is coming with us. And please, keep it quiet! I don't want the whole castle gossiping about it before I get a chance to inform the Council."

"As you wish, my King."

Ferris acknowledged the gesture with a nod.

"Do me a favor and take some rest, my dear? Now that everything is taken care of?" Broc addressed Kelly again.

"Yes, dear. Don't you worry about me. Not when you have a Council meeting coming up."

Ferris looked at her more carefully now, as much as the dim torch light allowed. Could he detect a slight flush in her cheeks? A curvier figure than he remembered? Perhaps the changes he'd first noticed in her weren't due to the years that had passed but for a more specific reason. And the remarks Broc had made…. Of course! She was with child!

A fresh wave of guilt welled up in his chest. An invasion couldn't come at a worse time. If Kelly, or her unborn child were harmed in any way…. How would he live with himself?

After Broc had left the two of them, Ferris failed to keep track of where Kelly was taking him.

She kept on talking to him, asking him things, but he could barely answer. His mind was working on just one problem right now: how to prevent the worst from happening.

How to keep Kelly and her new world safe from the harm he had unleashed upon them.

It killed him that he had no solution to that particular problem.

———◆———

As Eryn reached Rhea's quarters, she hesitated just for a moment. In the end, logic won out. Rhea needed to know what had happened, without any delay. Whether or not she'd be happy about it was secondary.

She knocked on the door and waited for any answer. Nothing.

Again, Eryn knocked louder, and called out as well. "General Rhea, I have news."

Finally, someone stirred inside.

"What could it possibly be, at this time of night?" a male voice complained.

"Shit," Eryn cursed under her breath.

Of course, Rhea wasn't alone. Her mate, Saras, was with her.

As awkward as that made things, there was no turning back for Eryn. Rhea had chided her once for being kept out of the loop. She wouldn't make the same mistake again.

No, but I keep on failing to follow through on Rhea's orders to kill the warlock, Eryn thought bitterly.

Even if it had turned out for the best under these current circumstances.

"I have important news for General Rhea. It cannot wait."

"Very well," Saras said, as he opened the door to reveal his immortality in full glory.

Eryn tried her best to keep her eyes to herself, but the dragon shifter had made that nearly impossible. Naked, save for a towel of sorts wrapped tightly around his most pertinent bits, Eryn began to understand just a little bit why Rhea accepted a lot of the dragon's nonsense.

He was something else. But as good-looking as he was, he had nothing on the warlock. Shit, had she actually just meant that?

"Uhm." Eryn cleared her throat. "Where is she? I mean, where's the General?"

Saras grinned at her and stepped aside. "Why don't you enter our humble quarters, my dear. And you'll find out for yourself."

"Eryn, it's quite alright. You can come in," Rhea called out from further inside the room. She looked much more respectable, standing beside the bed in her simple linen nightgown. No frills or lace for the General, Eryn observed.

Again, she tried not to stare, but her curiosity got the better of her. The furnishings inside the room were an eclectic mix of old and new. Antique weaponry adorned the walls, which stood out starkly against the heavy, lavish drapes that surrounded the luxurious poster bed. It was obvious that the weapons had been Rhea's choice. And it was likely Saras who enjoyed a bit more opulence....

After a thousand years spent in the castle dungeons for whatever reason, Eryn couldn't fault him for that.

"Tell me you have good news?" Rhea's tone was gruff; it made Eryn flinch.

"Right. So, I went down into the dungeons," Eryn started, then shot a sideways look toward Saras.

"I know.... You were supposed to kill the warlock in his sleep. Just pretend I'm not here," Saras said.

Eryn glanced at Rhea again, who nodded and gestured at her to carry on.

Kind of hard to do, when you're so damn.... naked!

Not that Eryn was a prude. Transforming in and out of their human forms required the islanders to take off their clothing quite regularly. That much she was used to. But he was Rhea's mate, which made things awkward now.

Wonder what the warlock would look like. How different would he be?

Focus, Eryn!

"So, did you kill the bastard or not?" Rhea said.

Eryn averted her gaze. "No, but please hear me out."

From the corner of her eye, Eryn saw Rhea folding her arms across her chest.

Eryn took a deep breath. *Best get to the point!*

"I overheard a conversation between Kelly and him."

"What? Our lovely mortal queen, conspiring with the enemy?" Saras exclaimed. "Now things are getting *really* exciting."

"And what exactly was this conversation about?" Rhea asked.

"It turns out, she had a brother, back on the mainland. He came here to find her. They're siblings!" Eryn explained.

"The warlock and the witch." Saras rubbed his hands together. "Of course! It makes perfect sense. So, what were they talking about? Are they going to try and destroy us from within?"

Eryn rolled her eyes and shot him a nasty look. He might be the General's consort, but she didn't care anymore. He was starting to get on her nerves again, just like he had during the Council meeting earlier.

"Excuse him and his rather unusual sense of humor," Rhea remarked wryly.

"Well, sorry, but when you get to be over a thousand years old, very few things tend to excite you anymore," Saras said with a smile.

Eryn shook her head. "All I know is, the warlock is the queen's brother. The king arrived just as I was leaving, so he's aware of the situation. I don't know for sure what any of it means yet."

"Probably a good thing you didn't kill him, huh? That would have been awkward. *Oh, sorry, Queen Kelly, I didn't realize he was your brother!"* Saras' laughter echoed against the walls of the room.

For all the ridiculous things that had come out of his mouth so far, this was the first thing Eryn could agree with.

"And you, too, my dear. I'm pretty sure you'd have been sent to the dungeons for that. But don't worry. I would have waited for you," Saras said in a much gentler tone as the couple shared a look of understanding.

Just what it was they shared beyond sex, Eryn had no idea.

Maybe one day…. With the right man…. How I wish it could be the queen's brother.

This was hardly the time to think about all of that.

"So, how do we proceed?" Eryn interrupted her own illicit thoughts.

CHAPTER SEVEN

———◆———

Although still plagued by guilt, Ferris was glad to spend a little time alone with Kelly before the inevitable Council meeting.

He followed her through the endless corridors of the castle. Even when he had managed to get an audience with King Harrold in *his* castle, he hadn't seen a structure as large and confusing as this one.

"How do you find your way around?" he wondered.

Kelly laughed. "That's what I thought when I first got here. You get used to it. And…. here we are!"

She gestured at him to be quiet and carefully opened the door. Ferris took a moment to let his eyes adjust. The light inside was dim, with only a small candle lit on a small table at the far side of the room.

There was a huge, empty bed toward the right of it, presumably for Kelly and her husband, and a much smaller cot toward the left. If Ferris held his breath, he could hear the deep breaths of a child, sleeping.

Kelly stepped inside to check on him. It was a beautiful sight. Her expression was full of love as she gazed down on the boy.

Ferris wanted nothing more than to see him too. Would he have her eyes? Her fiery red hair? But to disturb such careless bliss would be too cruel.

He joined his sister at the child's bedside. Kelly leaned over and was just about to touch the boy when Ferris stopped her, shaking his head.

"Don't wake him yet."

He was beautiful. Curly hair—Ferris couldn't make out the color in this light. Perfectly symmetrical features and a cute button nose. Like a little angel.

"Little Finlay," Ferris whispered.

Never in his wildest dreams had he expected anything like this. Not only was his sister happy with her supposed captors, she had a beautiful son now too, and another child on the way. And to think that he had worked for years to try to destroy these lands, when what they really needed was his protection.

He breathed in deeply, but a tear still stung in his eye. Regret. How familiar he was starting to become with that feeling.

Ferris balled his fists and tried to control his breathing to keep calm. He couldn't let anything bad happen to this little man. Not on his watch.

They continued to stand in the darkened room in silence, watching as the boy slept.

Would he ever know how it felt to have a son of his own? If these Isles by some miracle survived the threat from the mainland, only then would he have the chance to make that dream a reality.

Strange, how quickly things could change. For so many

years his sole focus had been to get Kelly back. Only now that they were reunited and he'd met her family, as unconventional as it was, had the thought even crossed his mind. A family of his own. With a woman he could care for, just as Kelly's husband seemed to care for her.

A distant dream indeed.

A careful knock on the door interrupted their little moment with Finlay.

Kelly turned to him and whispered. "It must be time for the meeting. Will you join us?"

Ferris nodded.

Ferris was still in turmoil when he was led into a great big hall, filled with impossibly large wooden benches and tables. Remnants of a feast adorned the tables. Empty plates and pitchers galore, with a couple of sleeping soldiers to boot.

He could only guess it was time for the so-called Council meeting. And apparently he had gone from prisoner to guest of honor in under an hour.

Kelly and he waited in silence as Broc ordered some men to clear out the drunken soldiers. What was about to be discussed wasn't meant for everyone. Only select eyes and ears would be allowed inside.

"Where is everyone else?" Broc demanded.

A few guards scurried about, then whispered

something in response.

"Well, wake them up, then! Your King commands it!" Broc ordered.

Kelly walked up to him and rested her hand on his arm, which seemed to calm him down only slightly. These two had a very unusual dynamic indeed.

Once again, Ferris didn't just feel like he wasn't needed here, he was overcome with the same deep, dark regret he had felt watching Finlay sleep.

If only he had accepted Kelly's fate, like the villagers had tried to tell him all those years ago. If only he hadn't tried to mess with things he didn't understand. Then they wouldn't be in this situation now.

Calm down. Beating yourself up isn't going to do anyone any good, Kelly's voice said.

Ferris flinched and looked at her, then at Broc, and at her again. She hadn't said that aloud, had she? Nobody else seemed to have heard her.

Oh, is that not how your magic works? Kelly asked.

It was her, right there in his mind. The look in her eye confirmed as much.

No…. no it is not, Ferris thought. *You can read minds?*

Kelly smiled in response.

I wish I could read minds sometimes…. Ferris momentarily glanced at Broc again. *Can you read all their minds too? Anyone of your choosing?*

Kelly nodded briefly. *That's how it started out. By now, I can do a lot more than just that.*

Ferris couldn't believe it. He'd never met anyone else with magical powers. So naturally, he'd assumed that his unique skills were the norm. To find out that different people could possess different ones…. Well it strangely made sense now that he thought about it.

What can you do? Kelly seemed to ask.

Ferris scanned the room for any sign of an animal so he could demonstrate. A cat, or perhaps a rodent, scurrying about in the scraps of food left behind on the floor. There were none.

I can leave my body for short periods of time and control animals.

Kelly frowned briefly. *What a curious power to have.*

It can be useful.

Their silent conversation was interrupted by the arrival of what Ferris presumed to be the rest of the Council. A handful of haggard-looking old men entered. They were still unnaturally tall like their younger counterparts, although their advanced age had shrunk them somewhat. Their long beards and thinning hair matched the gray of their ankle length cloaks.

Behind them, some more people arrived, men as well as women. Not a familiar face among them, until finally, the last to enter the hall and close the doors behind her.

That same woman. The one who had come to kill him in his cell.

They shared a quick stare of recognition, but neither said a word.

Instead, the woman tried to ignore him and joined another, much sterner-looking female in leather armor and not much else in terms of clothing, toward the left of the King. The latter gave him a foul look. Presumably he had finally come face-to-face with the person who'd wanted him dead. His captor's commander.

What a strange society this was. Where his sister was queen, and women fought and led in battle alongside their male counterparts, seemingly as equals. Most mainlanders would scoff at the mere thought, but Ferris found it strangely enchanting.

"Finally! Let us begin," Broc said. "I've called you back so soon because we've had a new development. And you will have noticed that there's a new face amongst us."

Everyone's eyes were on him immediately, the woman he'd met already included. And for a moment, it was her gaze which made him forget why he was even here.

What the hell is he *doing here?* Eryn had a hard time keeping her eyes off the warlock.

Sure, he had turned out to be the queen's brother, but to see him here apparently attending a Council Meeting was still unexpected. Presence at these meetings was an honor bestowed on only select inhabitants of Black Mountain. Only the king's closest and most trusted men and women were chosen to attend.

Hell, it had taken Eryn years by Rhea's side to earn herself a spot.

Royal privilege, she thought.

And worse still, he was looking at her. Still no sign of his presence in her mind, but what if he was just waiting for the right time to strike? His loyalties might have shifted now that he was reunited with his long-lost sister, but Eryn still feared what he might find in her thoughts.

Unspeakable things she couldn't even admit to herself.

Inappropriate glimpses that had entered her imagination since their first meeting, which had never truly gone away.

In a way it had been more bearable when she thought he was the enemy. She could've held onto the idea that sooner or later he'd be dead or banished, and she wouldn't have to deal with these feelings anymore.

If he was now their ally, that made things a million times worse.

He was gorgeous, though. And the way he looked at her made her weak in the knees.

How could she justify thinking that way of the queen's brother? She'd been born into simple circumstances. That she'd worked her way up under Rhea's guidance hardly mattered. She would never be worthy of him.

She only half listened to the King explain certain details she'd already overheard down in the dungeons, distracted as she was by her ever more complicated feelings towards Queen Kelly's brother.

"No offense to our Queen's judgment, but I would advise caution," Rhea's voice echoed around the room.

Eryn forced herself to listen now. If only she could stop *thinking* so much.

"I for one am not convinced we should be having this discussion…. openly." Rhea was once again displeased with how the King was handling things and she wasn't mincing her words this time.

"Hear, hear." Yorrick jumped to Rhea's support, which was unusual. The man rarely spoke much during these meetings.

Eryn stole a glance at Queen Kelly, who had placed her hands squarely on her hip in clear defiance of Rhea's remarks. Finally, some much needed distraction.

"Say what you will, but I know I can trust my own brother!"

"Sure, once upon a time. But how much has changed since the last time you saw one another?" Rhea argued.

"Time can change a person," Yorrick added.

Eryn glanced at him and noticed he was eying the warlock suspiciously.

Meanwhile, the two women stared each other down. This wasn't going to turn out into an altercation, was it? And just who would win such a fight? Rhea was physically superior, but magic trumped all.

"You seem to forget that I can read minds," the queen spoke defiantly.

"And you seem to forget that he has some powers of his own. Perhaps he's been using them on us all already."

"Enough!" King Broc intervened. "I'll accept no more of this bickering. Whether or not he's trustworthy is secondary to the real issue at hand. He had nothing to gain from informing us about the incoming ships; all it does is help us. And we're unprepared!"

Eryn's heart skipped a beat. There was an attack brewing? Just how much of the king's earlier announcement had she missed while obsessing over the newcomer?

"Fine," Rhea said. "Let's assume the information is accurate for a moment."

"Thank you!" the king said.

"Can't he just call them off? He's their supposed leader, yes?" Rhea asked.

Eryn looked at the warlock again, and then back at the king and Rhea.

"He's simply an envoy to King Harrold of the Mainland," the queen explained.

"Does he not speak for himself?" Rhea asked. "What's your name, anyway?"

"Ferris. My name is Ferris," the warlock spoke up for the first time.

Eryn found herself mesmerized again. Such a strange name.

"My sister is right. I'm here under orders. Sure, I had a hand in organizing this excursion. But the King of the

Mainland would have never given me his blessings, or his support, if he didn't believe in the cause himself. The lottery is a sore point for many of our people and that's why they're willing to fight."

"Lottery?" Rhea frowned and turned to face King Broc.

"He means the Reaping. The mainlanders aren't happy giving up their daughters anymore," Kelly spoke up instead.

Everyone was quiet for a moment.

Eryn looked at them all one by one. Rhea, Yorrick, even the king; they all remained silent. Was no one going to voice the obvious?

"My King, my Queen, General Rhea," Eryn interrupted the silence.

"Yes?" Rhea snapped.

"Well, do we strictly *need* the Reaping ritual anymore?" Eryn asked. "If that's what's standing between our safety and a war we can't possibly win?"

"Nobody said we couldn't possibly win it," the King said.

Rhea looked at him sideways, as did Eryn. Perhaps not, but everyone was thinking exactly that.

Uri banged his staff onto the ground, attracting everyone's attention, and ran his hand through his long, thinning beard. "The Reaping exists for a reason. It was only through fresh stock that our people came back from the brink of extinction!"

Eryn nodded. "Right. Back in the day when our numbers had dwindled so much, we were but a handful of families left. I've read the history. But our circumstances have changed since then. And if we lose this war, there will be no Reapings to help us recover. We'll be done for."

Again, everyone was silent. Even Uri did not argue further. Her logic was sound, wasn't it?

Eryn noticed Yorrick staring at her. Perhaps she could count on his support at least?

"Do you suggest we sit down with these mainlanders and offer them a deal right away? They'll sense our weakness and strike anyway," Rhea spoke up first.

Eryn opened her mouth to respond, but didn't get the chance.

Everyone assembled started talking over each other; the Elders in one corner, King Broc and Rhea in another, with Yorrick trying and failing to get a word in between.

The only people who didn't speak aloud were Kelly and her brother. But from the looks they were giving each other, Eryn was certain even they were having an animated exchange of their own.

She sunk down against one of the tables and stared at her feet. These arguments weren't going to get them anywhere. They had no way of knowing how much time they had left.

Eryn gave it one minute, even two, all the while shaking her head as she got angrier and angrier. Etiquette was all fine and well, but this ruckus was getting to her.

She couldn't take it any longer, picked up one of the empty earthenware pitchers from the table, and threw it with all her might into the floor, where it shattered into hundreds of pieces.

"Enough already!" she roared.

Everyone stopped talking. *Shit. Do I apologize?*

Eryn straightened herself. To hell with it. She didn't normally have a temper, but this was justified.

"While we're standing here debating about what not to do, our enemy is gearing up for battle!" she said. "Am I right?" she addressed only Ferris this time.

He nodded his head. "They're already on the way."

Eryn pointed at him and nodded as well. "There. So rather than get in our own way, we must prepare ourselves as well. If my idea was dumb, by all means let's come up with something better."

From the corner of her eye, Eryn thought she could detect the hint of a smile on Ferris' lips. It caused a flutter in her chest, which made her nervous all over again.

At least someone was pleased. Most of the others just looked frustrated.

She'd get to hear all about authority and respect from Rhea later. In all her years attending these meetings, never once had she even thought about doing something like this.

Perhaps she was just tired of being ordered around. Or perhaps she needed a proper crisis to come into her own.

"Eryn has a point," Rhea said after a long pause.

The rest of the Council seemed to slowly come around too. Or they were too stunned to argue.

"But we cannot capitulate from the outset," Rhea added. "One must always try to negotiate from a position of power, not one of weakness."

King Broc turned to her and nodded. "True, but how do you suggest we achieve that? If we engage them…." It seemed he didn't want to finish that sentence.

Silence, again. Until the most unlikely person in the room started to speak as well.

"That might be something I can help with," Ferris said.

Eryn swallowed hard upon looking at him again. How could he have such a profound effect on her? If it wasn't magic, then what was it?

CHAPTER EIGHT

erris hadn't doubted it when he first saw her, but this meeting had confirmed it. The woman, Eryn, had some guts. Almost everyone in attendance, except maybe the old men in cloaks, were her superiors. But rather than stand by in silence, she'd made her voice heard.

He was in awe.

But now that he'd come out in her support, he had to follow through and convince the others that he *could* be trusted.

"I don't know if you know this, but the mainlanders are a superstitious lot. Most fear the unknown more than anything," Ferris said.

The islanders nodded, with some hesitation.

"Kelly and I have powers that will send grown men running."

Kelly smiled at him. *Not just grown* men, *actually.*

Ferris frowned. *Tell me that story another time, sis.*

"Right, so you think the two of you alone can hold off a whole fleet of ships?" King Broc asked.

Not quite, it was actually a lot simpler than that. And so obvious, now that he thought about it.

"I can command the weather," Ferris announced.

A whisper traveled the room, but most of the giants

still looked confused at what he was trying to tell them.

"Well, that is to say, I can summon clouds, thunder, mist, that kind of thing," he added.

"Exactly how much cloud and such can you summon?" Rhea asked.

"Enough to hide Black Mountain from view?" Eryn interjected.

Ferris smiled and nodded. "Give me a few minutes and you won't see each other through the dense fog I'll conjure."

"We'll manage just fine," Rhea remarked. "But the humans won't see a thing!"

How's that? Ferris thought and glanced over at Kelly.

It's a long story. One for another day. She smiled. *Nice skill. Can you command lightning, too?*

How did you guess?

She smiled even wider now. *Let's just say perhaps that's where our powers overlap a little.*

Ferris looked around the room and found Eryn already staring at him. Earlier she had impressed him, and now it seemed he had gotten her attention too.

Oh, you like her! Kelly's voice echoed in his mind.

Stop it! Get out of my head!

When he looked at her again, he noticed Eryn was now embroiled in an animated discussion with Rhea. Their voices were hushed, so he could not make out what they were talking about.

"Very well," King Broc spoke up again. "It sounds like

we have a plan."

For the first time since realizing his mistake, Ferris also felt a glimmer of hope. If he had brought this danger upon them all, it was only right that his powers should help their cause. It would take a significant amount of energy and focus to hide an entire island, but he was up for the challenge.

Failure was not an option.

"Rhea, you'll get our troops ready. We'll have archers positioned on the fortifications. Eryn's lookouts will start patrolling on overlapping shifts starting right now. Uri, if there's anything in the scriptures, anything that could help dealing with the mainlanders going forward…. But we won't negotiate just yet. Perhaps we can achieve victory without having to give up on the Reaping after all."

"Yes, my King," one of the old men replied.

The two women simply nodded in agreement.

"Get to work, everyone!" the king said.

Everyone moved into action.

That's it? Ferris had to wonder just how they were going to prepare for such a large threat with so little instruction on the king's part. And just how were they planning to fight effectively in zero visibility?

Ferris had all these questions and more, when he noticed Rhea taking the king aside for more hushed conversation. Perhaps a lot of the actual planning would take place behind closed doors. Away from him, just in case.

Fair enough. Just because he'd turned out to be Kelly's brother didn't mean they had to trust him immediately. He wouldn't, were the tables turned.

No matter how much he offered to help, this whole mess was still his fault.

The cloaked old men were starting to leave, as were most of the other attendees of the meeting. He positioned himself further away from Rhea and the king, leaving them to their secret conversation, while Kelly remained by her husband's side.

With nowhere to be and nothing to do, Ferris simply watched the activity around him, until Eryn tried to slip past him.

So much left unsaid between them.

He caught her by the arm. "Not so fast."

She gave him a stern look, then stared down at his hand on her arm.

"I have to get my lookout squad ready. You heard the king's orders. We're about to enter our first war in years, thanks to you," Eryn said.

Although her tone was flat and emotionless, her words still stung. She had voiced exactly what he'd been thinking all along.

Ferris looked away briefly, but he did not release his grip. They were about equally matched in height, but she was strong. A formidable fighter, as their first meeting had proved beyond a doubt. If she wanted to, she'd already have freed herself.

Still, there she stood, with her gaze fixed now on the empty space between them.

"I need to explain my actions. I need you to know that my intentions were pure," Ferris said. Just why he was telling her this, he wasn't sure.

What would she care about his motivations? If she paid him no attention at all, he could not blame her. Still, he cared what she thought of him.

And she seemed willing to listen. So, he continued.

"It was all for her, you see. Growing up, it was the two of us, ever since our mother passed away. Kelly and I. She took care of me when I was little. And when I came home from my first job at sea, she was gone. Just like that. I couldn't accept it. I owed it to her to get her home safely. It's all I've been thinking about all these years."

Eryn pressed her lips together and glanced up at him for the briefest of moments.

"You were trying to do the right thing for her."

"Yes."

"How could you know the truth? That she had made a place for herself here. A family."

"How indeed. On the mainland we know very little of these Isles and the people on them. Nothing but scary stories told around campfires. Rumors in the dark."

Eryn shrugged. "Sounds like we both have a lot to learn about each other."

Ferris nodded. "And yet we have no time to learn it."

Their eyes met, and an eerie feeling overcame him. That same familiarity he'd felt the first time he laid eyes on her.

"Will you tell me now where I've seen you before? Unless it's a secret?"

A smile played briefly on her lips. Finally, some sign of humanity. Perhaps he was getting through to her now.

"Funnily, it *is* a secret, actually."

Ferris shook his head in feigned frustration. If she wanted to toy with him, fine. It was better than the alternative; having her ignore him, or hate him for putting them all in danger.

The last Council members passed them by, and just like that, her expression turned serious again.

"And I *really* do have to go now," she said.

Ferris relented. He'd said what needed to be said. Now it was up to her what she wanted to believe.

"Good luck," he said.

Eryn nodded, and just like that, she was gone.

Ferris checked the Hall and found that only Kelly and her husband were left inside.

"Can you really do what you told everyone?" King Broc asked.

Kelly frowned at him. "Of course he can! Why would he lie about that?"

Ferris raised his hand in a calming motion. "It's fine. I wouldn't trust me either. But yes. I'll be able to disguise us.

Your men have the home advantage. The incoming ships will be drifting around blindly."

"That's all I wanted to know. You'll be informed when we spot the ships," the king said.

Ferris nodded, then turned to his sister.

"Kelly," he said.

"Yes, Ferris?"

"This is going to sound like an odd request. But do you suppose I could go somewhere to rest until it is time?" He turned to face Broc again. "If it's alright with you, of course."

Broc shrugged and turned away from the two of them.

Kelly nodded. "You need rest to conserve your powers. As do I."

A very old and yet familiar warmth overcame him. He hadn't felt like this for years. For the first time in his adult life, he knew someone understood him inside and out.

"I've missed you, sis."

She smiled and placed her hand on his cheek. Like she used to do when he was just a boy. For a moment he was back in a simpler time. Back in West Hythe, in the little house they grew up in.

"I missed you too…. Now let's find you somewhere to stay," she said.

They left the hall and found themselves in yet another corridor, where Kelly turned around and called out for someone.

"Bree, are you around?"

A woman quite a bit taller than Kelly appeared. Her simple wardrobe and timid body language suggested she was a maidservant or worker here at the castle.

"Yes, my Queen?" The woman kept her head bowed as she spoke.

"This is my brother, Ferris. Can you prepare a room for him somewhere to rest? And, Bree?" Kelly paused.

"Yes?"

"No need to be so formal. We're only human."

The joke worked, judging from the little smile that appeared on Bree's lips.

Although he was starting to get used to the idea that Kelly was an actual monarch here, it was still odd to see her interacting with the other islanders, especially her underlings.

He thought *he'd* come a long way in his quest for revenge. She had come a whole lot further, almost entirely by chance.

"Follow me, Sir," Bree addressed him.

"Have a good rest," Kelly called after him.

He waved at her and followed Kelly's maidservant through the maze of corridors that was Black Mountain.

Although he had little idea just where she'd taken him, it wasn't a very long walk. Still, he was relieved when the door closed behind him, and he was alone again.

He did need rest, if he wanted to make sure his powers were at their peak for the upcoming fight. But he also needed something else. Clarity.

Ferris sat down on the center of the large bed that dominated the sparsely furnished room. Although simple, it was a thousand times more comfortable than most quarters he'd had the misfortune of living in all these years. Having a queen for a sister clearly had many benefits.

After folding his legs, he rested his hands on top of his knees, palms downward, and closed his eyes.

Breathe in. Hold. Breathe out.

Repeat.

Ferris cleared his mind of all the confusion and doubts that had haunted him since his capture.

Focus.

Magic was a funny thing. It had taken him years—and a lot of trial and error—to control it.

The main thing he'd learned during all that time was that mindset was everything. If he could imagine it, he could most likely do it, so long as it was something within his powers.

Controlling the weather was definitely something he could do. He'd used this trick so many times before. All he had to do was alter the scale.

Ferris breathed deeply again, and concentrated on his goal.

What did he want most in this world?

No longer did he meditate on revenge. He'd been so sure of himself all these years. His motivation had been set in stone, and yet it had taken only an hour or so for everything to change.

Now he had to find a new motivation. A new goal.

Safety. For Kelly and little Finlay.

He inhaled deeply and kept these two in his mind's eye, when very suddenly, a third person appeared in his vision.

Eryn.

Ferris opened his eyes and stared right into the flicker of the one candle that lit up this room.

"Eryn," he said to himself.

He had come here with a solitary aim.

That he wanted Kelly and Finlay to be safe was obvious. But if he was truly honest with himself, the thing he wanted most in this world….

Forgiveness.

It was only Eryn who could give that to him. It wouldn't matter if it came from anyone else.

And in time, if he was good enough, perhaps she could offer him more than that. Perhaps she could accept him the way Kelly had accepted Broc.

That was his new ultimate aim.

Ferris closed his eyes again and let his subconscious run free. The change was immediate. A rush of energy collected in his core. Now that he had found his ultimate desire, he felt more powerful than ever.

Perhaps love truly could conquer all.

CHAPTER NINE

ryn's little encounter with Ferris had sent her thoughts and emotions into turmoil all over again. Just when she had begun to get a grip on herself.

She had no idea why he'd wanted to talk to her of all people. She'd given him no reason to. Unless he had sensed how he made her feel. Could it be that the feeling was mutual?

Her heart jumped a few beats before she got herself under control. It didn't change anything. He was still related to the queen. And she was still unworthy.

Eryn forced herself back into action and all but ran out of the Great Hall. She'd barely made it out the door when she bumped into Yorrick.

"What was *that* all about?" Yorrick's stare made Eryn uncomfortable.

Now what did *he* want?

"What are you talking about?" she countered.

"The warlock. What did he want with you? Or rather, what did you want with him?"

Yorrick didn't seem his usual, calm self. Of course, they were all on edge, but she'd never known him to be the suspicious type.

"Oh, you know…. Unfinished business from the battle," Eryn said. Lying wasn't one of her strengths. "I was the one who captured him, if you remember."

"How about earlier tonight? Did you go see him in the dungeons to discuss this so-called unfinished business then too?"

"What in the world?" Eryn's heart sank. How did *he* know about that?

Her initial shock was quickly replaced with anger. "Have you been following me around, Yorrick?"

Now it was his turn to take a step back. His face turned ashen, and then bright red.

"I'm head of the Castle Guard. I ought to know what goes on in these walls!" His tone was defensive now.

She'd struck a nerve. In any case, there was no point denying she'd visited the warlock in his cell. Even the king and queen knew about that already.

"And I'm second in command to Rhea, our General. If I'm down in the dungeons, you can bet on it that I'm there with her blessing," Eryn snapped.

Yorrick took a step forward and loomed over her, but she didn't flinch or back down. How quickly things changed in these walls.

"I thought we were friends. Now you treat me as the enemy?" Eryn hissed.

Yorrick exhaled and broke eye contact. "Eryn…. That's not what I meant."

She continued to glare at him. What the hell was he thinking? Had he been following her around earlier also? All those little conversations out on the sea wall, the random encounters outside the library…. Had it all been an elaborate plan of his, rather than mere coincidence?

Rhea had noticed it and warned her. She had taken it as something else, professional rivalry between the Army and Castle Guard. But the truth had become apparent tonight.

"I'm only worried for your safety, Eryn!" Yorrick pleaded.

Eryn shook her head; she was having none of it. "You have a funny way of showing your concern."

"We *are* friends, though. Aren't we?" he asked.

She looked up again into his eyes, but made sure there was no warmth in her gaze. "Sure. Whatever you say. But that's *all* we'll ever be."

Eryn was still shaking with anger. If it was up to these menfolk, she'd *never* get the chance to carry out the King's orders tonight! She left Yorrick standing there in the corridor outside the Great Hall, and rushed off like she should have done immediately after the meeting.

She didn't have time for any of this nonsense. First Ferris tried to distract her with his apologies, and now Yorrick with…. She didn't even know what this was.

Between the king and queen letting an outsider attend the Council meeting, and everyone's apparent reluctance to try diplomacy on the enemy rather than fight them outright…. Had everyone on this rock gone insane, save for her?

By the time she reached her destination halfway across

the castle, she was still annoyed.

Eryn burst into the dormitory of her squad with little patience or compassion. Dawn would break shortly. There was no more time to lose.

"Wake up! All of you!"

Some of her people stirred quicker than others. The room stank of ale; her men had feasted heavily before going to bed.

"This isn't a joke. Get up. Your services are required immediately!" Eryn shouted.

Finally, everyone was up in their cots and rubbing their eyes.

"Mistress Eryn, what's going on?" The same young eagle who had initially found the human ship was first on his feet.

Very well, Eryn would brief him first, then. The others would fall in line soon enough.

"We are under immediate threat. The ship you spotted yesterday wasn't the only one coming," Eryn said.

The young man's eyes widened; she couldn't be sure whether with shock or excitement.

Some of the more senior members of her squad joined the two of them.

"We'll need to patrol day and night," one of them said.

Eryn nodded. "Overlapping shifts. We cannot afford to let the enemy slip past unseen."

It didn't take long for even the laziest of the lot to jump into action.

Only then could Eryn breathe easy. She had done her part. Her squad would be in the air imminently. Nobody could escape their gaze now.

————•◆•————

After whipping her squad into shape, Eryn was intercepted right outside the dorm room.

"Oh, here you are." Rhea pulled her aside by her arm.

"Now that the *humans* are busy, it's time to have a real conversation."

Eryn blinked a few times. This was it. She was going to get an earful about her conduct during the Council Meeting. Unless Rhea wanted to interrogate her about her little chat with Ferris earlier?

"About?" Eryn asked with a heart full of trepidation.

"We discussed what we could in front of everyone, but I can't trust the warlock, no matter whose brother he is. The king agreed that we cover some things in private. The newcomer doesn't need to know everything. At least not yet."

Rhea was probably being a bit paranoid, but that wasn't any of Eryn's business. She was just glad the woman wasn't shouting at her. Yet. "Right."

"Come along."

Rhea marched off, and Eryn did her best to keep up. "Where are we going?"

"View Point."

Away from prying eyes and sensitive ears, and with the best views of the surrounding seas possible. Good choice.

When they got there, the king was already waiting, his hands on the railing as he peered out over the sea. Although his expression didn't show it, Eryn could almost sense his tension.

"We're here," Rhea said.

King Broc turned abruptly. Had they startled him?

"Good. Let's begin."

Eryn listened in silence as Rhea and Broc laid out their plans for the battle. They would be outnumbered for sure. And although the islanders were much stronger than their human counterparts in hand-to-hand combat, superior weaponry from the mainland could tip the scales even further in their favor.

If they couldn't be stronger, they had to be smarter.

"We will use the fog to our advantage and set sail to join the battle from the other side. Fight them on two fronts," Rhea said.

Eryn thought about it for a moment. "We have one of their ships. They won't come to know it's us until it's too late."

Rhea nodded. "That's exactly what I thought."

I knew that captured ship was going to come in handy.

"For this reason, I will need you to lead the troops on ground," Rhea said.

Eryn glanced up at the general, then at the king, then

back again. "You don't want me on the ship?"

Rhea shook her head. "The men need someone to look up to. You're my most senior officer on the ground."

It made sense, logically. Still Eryn could not deny her disappointment. This was exactly the sort of task *she* should have been given. As general, Rhea should be with the rest of her troops, commanding them, motivating them.

Her failure to carry out Rhea's orders had brought this on her. Eryn was being left behind.

"Any objections?" Rhea asked. Her tone betrayed that there was only one correct answer.

"No. that's fine."

Broc took a step in her direction and placed his hand on her shoulder. This was probably the first time the king had ever touched her, so there was no missing the significance in his gesture.

"I will be up here, overseeing the battle. If you need anything, you need only signal me."

Eryn averted her gaze. "Thank you, my King."

"That's enough now. She's become arrogant enough as it is," Rhea grumbled. "Unless you've forgotten what happened at the meeting."

Broc smiled bitterly. "It was rather hard to forget or ignore. But the girl has sense."

"We can trust you with this, can't we?"

Trust her with keeping up morale at the front line and

lead the clash onshore? If he put it like that, perhaps it wasn't a punishment after all.

Eryn took a deep breath. "Absolutely, my King. I will not disappoint you."

"Once the fog sets, all bets are off. We won't hide behind these human faces if the humans reach our shores, understand? They won't know what hit them," King Broc said.

Eryn nodded. "Yes, I understand."

"Now run along and get yourself ready. I'll collect a handful of experienced fighters to join me on my mission at sea," Rhea said.

Eryn still felt a little sore for being left out. Or perhaps she was nervous about acting the leader? It was easy enough to boss around a bunch of inexperienced scouts…. She'd have a harder time with the senior soldiers.

But, as she had proved during the meeting, she wouldn't let anyone push her around anymore.

"Thank you for placing this trust in me," Eryn said.

"Yes, yes. Enough already," Rhea brushed her off.

Eryn nodded and left. As the door leading to the View Point closed slowly behind her, she could faintly overhear Rhea and Broc over the howling winds outside.

"I hope that warlock delivers," Rhea grumbled. "And Eryn, too."

"And if not, can we count on his help?" Broc asked.

"I'll talk to him, but I can't make any promises."

Eryn frowned. What on earth were they talking about

now? Still, none of her business. She carried on down the stairs and headed straight for the armory.

With nothing better to do, and nowhere else to be, she would spend the last moments of peace there. Surrounded by the smell of worn leather and polished iron, she would make sure her weapons and armor were in order.

But once the door closed behind her and she was alone amongst all these trappings of war, it wasn't her equipment she was thinking about.

She still made sure to check everything, but once that was done, and she sat idle, with her hands folded in her lap.

There was only one thing on her mind.

It wasn't the immense responsibility that rested on her now. It wasn't even the very real danger that many islanders, herself included, might not make it to the end of the upcoming fight.

Her thoughts were much simpler, and completely inappropriate. Like an unwanted guest, *he* had made himself at home in her mind from the moment he'd set foot on this island.

No matter how hard she tried. Eryn couldn't stop thinking of Ferris.

Perhaps deep down, she knew that he was thinking about her too.

CHAPTER TEN

The rumble of the war horn shook Black Mountain to its foundations. A little trickle of dust made its way down from the ceiling and onto the floor.

Eryn was ready, but the sound still made her skin crawl. She'd only heard it once before, when she had been freshly enlisted by Rhea. Years ago, during the first great battle with the Sea Folk; that was the last time the horn had sounded in these walls.

This time she wasn't a novice any longer. She would be in charge of the fighters stationed on the lower sea wall. That was the first point of contact between Black Isle's army and the enemy.

Over the years she hadn't just become a little more mature, but hopefully wiser and more experienced as well. All of these, and more. She would need to do a proper job today.

But just because she was in charge didn't mean she wouldn't pick up a weapon herself. That's not how things worked here. The human ships were coming, and on them, at least a thousand men, all armed to the teeth.

Eryn would fight just like any other soldier.

With the help of Ferris' magic, they would strike the enemy hard in an attempt to scare them off. To quash this invasion before it even got started.

There was no talk of compromise or diplomacy any longer. Rhea had gotten her way and convinced the king that brute force was the way forward. The general herself would flank the enemy using one of their own ships and try to take out as many as possible before they even reached the shore.

Eryn didn't like it, but could do nothing about it now but follow her orders.

All she knew was by the end of it, she'd be a battle virgin no longer. She'd take a life—many lives—before the day was done.

So be it.

For her people, for these Isles, she could do anything.

If she failed, she didn't just let Rhea and the King down, after all. She'd let herself down more than anything. It was her moment to shine and to prove to everyone including herself that she was worthy of her rank.

She ran down the corridors leading to the Drawbridge and almost bumped into Saras.

"Hey. Ready to fight?" she asked in passing.

"What? Oh, I'm not going out there."

Eryn stopped in her tracks and looked back at the man, who continued to leisurely walk in the wrong direction. It looked almost like he was going for an afternoon stroll around the castle. Surely, he had heard the war horn just like everyone else?

"What do you mean you're not going? We're all going

into battle. Our future is at stake!"

"I'll be waiting this one out, my dear. I'm sure between Rhea and you, the Isles are in capable hands."

Did he even know what Rhea was up against? How she was putting her life at risk by jumping head first into the fight?

Eryn wanted to berate him. To release all her frustration right now, call him arrogant and short-sighted and all the rest of it.

But she swallowed it.

This anger would come in handy later.

What on earth did Rhea see in him? Or rather, how did she not see all the selfishness hidden beneath that flawless exterior? This man seemed to be Rhea's only weakness.

Speaking of weaknesses, at least *Ferris* was trying to help…. Even if he was an outsider and worse still, the Queen's brother…. But his intentions were pure and he wasn't running away from this fight like Saras was doing.

Eryn shook it off and proceeded through the Drawbridge and down to the sea wall.

They'd have to survive this fight with or without a dragon by their side.

Some archers had already assembled and spread out to their positions. And most of them did not look as fresh or as ready as she would want them to. They had waited for Rhea to join their side, not Eryn. She could almost sense their disappointment.

But Rhea wasn't coming.

This was the best they were going to get.

Not one for rousing speeches normally, Eryn straightened herself and took a deep breath. It was the moment of truth.

"Guys!" she called out to the archers who had already assembled. "Some of you are seeing all-out war for the first time, and some of you already know the horrors that lie in our not so distant future. But our people have survived every challenge, every conflict we were thrust into in the past. And we will survive today!"

Now that she'd started, Eryn was surprised how easily the words came to her.

"With magic on our side, we will prevail. We will crush the opposition. We'll make heads roll. We'll live to fight another day! What say you?" she called out.

"I say death to the enemy!" the senior-most soldier of the group responded. Their eyes met and she could see a glimmer of hope in him. Morale was everything. They might just get away with this. Despite being outnumbered, the Isles could be victorious after all.

Where was Ferris, anyway? From where would he perform his magic?

More importantly, would he make good on his promises at all?

Eryn shook off her own doubts and continued to play the crowd. "That's right! Now the rest of you. What say you?"

"Victory!" the soldiers roared.

"Very good! Back to your posts! We attack as soon as the fog sets in."

It felt good to be listened to. To be respected. She held on tight to her bow, determined to do these men and women proud. No guts, no glory.

But for now, they could only wait. Eryn kept her eyes fixed on the horizon, where the mainlander's ships had already appeared. It wouldn't be long now. There was none of the normal chatter amongst the soldiers. Everyone was focusing on the same thing. Waiting, anticipating, until the enemy would arrive.

It was the calm before the storm.

———◆———

On the eve of the battle, Ferris felt fully charged.

He knew he'd need every last reserve, every bit of untapped energy, to fulfill his promise to Kelly's new family.

And to prove his loyalty to Eryn.

But he was ready for it.

There was some arrogance to his excitement. After years of using his powers for selfish means, now he'd be able to help someone other than himself. And perhaps impress Eryn in the process? It was her reaction he was looking   forward to especially.

From motivating all his actions solely on Kelly, he was

now doing it equally for the three people most important to him: Kelly, Finlay and Eryn.

As soon as the horn sounded the arrival of the invading ships, a guard had fetched him from his new quarters and brought him down to the Drawbridge, where he waited for further instructions.

But in the coming and going of armed soldiers, nobody took note. No one so much as approached him.

Luckily, he spotted Eryn in the distance. She had already made her way down toward the sea wall that surrounded the whole island. There she stood, completely still, with her back turned toward the castle. As he followed her path, he scanned his surroundings. Archers dotted the entire coastline. Their spread was thin, but perhaps these were all the fighters they had. The only protection for all these fighters were the fortifications of the wall they stood on.

There wasn't a bit of vegetation within sight. The entire island was practically barren, with the castle serving as a great big target for the incoming ships' cannons. The sort of weaponry he'd seen so far on this side of the fight wasn't nearly as advanced. Swords, axes and bows. Unless they were hiding a secret weapon somewhere, he wasn't particularly impressed. Physical strength was only part of the equation in combat.

Good thing he was on their team. Without his help, they wouldn't stand a chance against the military might of the mainland.

He looked up and saw eagles circling overhead. They bore an eerie resemblance to the one he'd spotted above his ship barely a day earlier. Funny. Had they trained these animals to help in their defense, as an early warning system perhaps?

Clearly there was a lot about these Isles and its people that he did not yet know. They kept their secrets closely guarded, even or especially from him.

No matter, he'd figure it out in time.

"How far out are they?" Ferris asked Eryn as he reached her side.

She looked at him for just a moment longer than necessary before pointing at the horizon. "There."

Ferris squinted, but he couldn't see anything.

"You have extraordinary vision," Ferris mumbled.

"I know," Eryn spoke in a matter-of-fact tone, but then stole another glance in his direction. "What's your plan?"

She was trying to hide it, but Ferris was picking up on the subtle signs now. She was as eager to see him in action as he was.

"Wait for them to just about get into view—*my view*— then blanket the enemy and the island in fog. The rest is up to you and your fighters."

"Sounds good to me."

Ferris continued to observe her, but she did not face him anymore. Her sole focus was now on the enemy. Here she stood, waiting to fight an opponent that outnumbered the islanders probably three or four to one.

Yet there wasn't a hint of fear or hesitation about her. What a formidable woman she was.

Ferris felt it best not to make further conversation. If all went according to plan, there would be plenty of time for that later.

If not…. then it didn't really matter, did it?

He did, however, make a promise to himself.

If they got out of this fight alive, and his loyalties were no longer in question, he would proposition her.

Returning to his homeland was no longer an option. Not when Kelly and his nephew were here, and he'd actively fought against King Harrold.

If the islanders would have him, he would try to make a life here for himself. He could only hope that Eryn was willing to share his future with him.

Because it was obvious to him now that he would never meet another woman like her. Her bravery impressed him greatly. In her, he saw qualities he wished for himself but which perhaps he had not yet managed to attain.

Eryn could be an opponent most dangerous, ruthless and willing to do what had to be done no matter how difficult. That's as far as their similarities went. And yet she had a capacity for mercy and forgiveness which he craved for himself.

Perhaps with her guidance, he would be worthy of a

woman like her.

Eryn cleared her throat beside him. "Can't you see them clearly yet? They'll be within our range soon."

Ferris peered out over the choppy waters. Indeed, the ships had come into view.

This was his moment.

He tilted his head to gaze at the clear sky one last time, before closing his eyes fully and retreating into his mind. A low rumble of thunder could be heard overhead, which made him smile.

You could smell the dampness in the air.

He could see it in his imagination now; he didn't even need to open his eyes to confirm. His magic was working and it was more powerful than ever before.

Dense fog covered everything, from the ships to the archers to the hills and castle behind them.

The invaders were now completely blind.

CHAPTER ELEVEN

———◆———

Eryn tried not to let Ferris' appearance distract her from the task at hand. The only thing disturbing the silence as they waited was the ever-increasing thump of her heart.

Whether it was nerves or excitement, she could not tell anymore. Neither did it matter.

Her instincts kicked in fast. She didn't consciously choose fight or flight. On her mind was only one thing: victory.

True to his word, as the ships approached, a mysterious fog crept up from the sea, surrounding everything and everyone.

Eryn turned around to see the extent of it. It took her breath away.

Even the worst weather these Isles had seen could not have disguised them this well.

She glanced at Ferris. He stood absolutely still, with his head tilted up toward the sky and his eyes shut. His arms were at a forty-five-degree angle to his body, with his palms facing upward. There was a slight tremble in his lip: remnants of words, not meant for anyone but himself and whatever higher power had granted him this magic.

It was probably too subdued for the human eye to see, but with her superior vision she could clearly make out a faint blue glow that surrounded his entire body.

His heartbeat was up at a feverish pace, and his breaths so shallow she could barely hear them over the crashing waves down below.

Whatever he was doing to make this happen, it was taking a toll on him.

"It better be worth it," she mumbled to herself and tightened her grip on her bow.

With an arrow lined up ready, she waited for the ships to get close enough for her to choose her first victim.

"Archers! If you have a shot, take it," she ordered.

"For victory!" one of the soldiers further down the wall called out.

"For glory!" the others responded.

A brief smile crept over Eryn's lips. This wasn't so bad, being a leader.

Hardly a minute passed before the first arrow ripped through the fog and implanted itself in the chest of an unsuspecting enemy soldier. He sunk to the ground so quickly, nobody else on board seemed to have any idea. Of course, they were at a severe disadvantage. The humans couldn't see much of anything.

One down, nine-hundred-and-ninety-nine to go, Eryn thought to herself.

She squinted and chose her own target. There was no time to think about the right or wrong of it all. She let go.

Nine-hundred-and-ninety-eight.

After this slow start, all the remaining archers let loose

as well. The enemy took a heavy battering of arrows, each shot with uncanny precision. It started off as easy as shooting at the practice range. But just as soon as the humans realized what they had sailed into, things became more challenging.

Their targets were no longer stationary, and many sought shelter behind various obstacles on board their ships. Some of them even started to return fire. So far, they were ineffective, blind as they were.

All the while, the enemy ships continued to approach ever closer. But the waters were treacherous. Sharp rocks dotted the coastline.

Soon enough, the first of many ran ashore. As soon as they felt the shudder, and heard the wooden hull groaning and cracking open against the unforgiving granite rock, the enemy soldiers started to abandon ship. Once again, it was open season on them.

Kill or be killed.

Eryn lost count soon thereafter.

A quick check on her men revealed that not one had fallen so far. They were doing well.

But Eryn's optimism was short-lived.

A flash of light lit up the mist quite some distance away, followed by a deafening rumble. Had Saras joined the fight after all?

Eryn leaned forward to get a better look, when a heavy object crashed into the island several feet behind her, causing the ground to shudder.

What on earth?

What was that which had been hurtled through the sky at them? And where exactly had it come from?

Whatever it was, it was impossibly fast and it must have been large and heavy as well. Too heavy for a mere human to lift at all, never mind be able to throw. Did they possess some secret weapon as well? Magic of their own, perhaps?

Eryn tried to catch her breath and scour the incoming ships for any sign of what might have caused it, when the same thing happened again.

The flash of light nearly blinded her, and made it hard for her to pinpoint its origin as well as trajectory.

"Archers! Forget everything else, aim at the shooting light before it goes off again!" Eryn shouted.

There was yet another flash in the distance, from another direction this time. The object hit a several feet to Eryn's left, crushing one of her men, and causing a whole section of fortified wall to crumble into the sea.

What was this witchcraft?

Eryn raised her bow and aimed. She never had the chance to shoot.

The impact hit her with such intensity, it forced all the wind out of her lungs.

Oh shit. I've been struck!

Eryn let out a muffled whimper as she sunk down onto her knees.

Devoid of air, she slipped away almost instantly.

All was going perfectly. Ferris was able to maintain his focus, and the fog did not let up.

Although his body was getting tired, he willed himself to carry on.

You can rest when you're dead.

The longer he carried on, the more distant he felt. A separation formed between his physical form and mind.

The weight of his body lifted off, as though he had started to float.

As soon as he felt it was safe, he opened his eyes. It was like he was looking down on himself, just like how it was when he took over another life form.

But this time, there was no other host around. There was just him, and his body, as two separate entities.

The islanders, including Eryn, carried on like nothing had changed. At least he assumed as much. She was the only one he could see, while the rest were hidden beyond the mist.

The fight seemed to be intensifying. He could hear the whistle of arrows being set loose on either side. Further away, the clanging of iron against iron had begun. Had the ships landed yet?

It wasn't long before the cannons started to fire, just as he had anticipated. But without being able to see their targets, they were firing blind. Hopefully the islanders would be able to neutralize the cannons before long, and without suffering too many losses.

Sure, there would be some casualties. The groans and cries of injured soldiers could be heard already, along with some more feral, almost animalistic cries. Ferris had no way of knowing what side the fallen belonged to.

War was a dirty game. One had to embrace the darkness in order to win.

At least the islanders could see, somewhat, allowing them to react. It was this little glimmer of hope that Ferris held onto. They were still at an advantage here.

Ferris floated higher above his body, only to find that now he couldn't see a damn thing anymore.

Focus, he thought.

Don't let go.

A nearby moan snapped him out of his trance. Within an instant, he was sucked back into his body and opened his actual, physical eyes. Just in time to see her fall.

"No! Eryn!" he called out and quickly bridged the gap between them.

The fog lifted as quickly as it had descended initially, but he took no note. All he could see was her ashen face, as he cradled her limp body in his arms.

Tears stung in his eyes, and a rage overcame him the likes of which he'd never felt before.

He'd lost someone once. Someone who had meant everything to him. Although he had Kelly back now, the wounds of that initial loss were ripped open again.

He wasn't about to go through that again.

Ferris rose to his feet and took in the full magnitude of what he was up against. He balled his fists so hard his whole body trembled.

Curses.

"You'll pay for this. You'll pay dearly!"

He raised his hands to the sky and screamed, releasing all his remaining energy, his newfound anger and pain, all at once.

The skies turned black as night, and the roar of thunder overwhelmed his senses.

Ferris started to shiver and shake. Every last hair on his body stood up straight. He inhaled deeply and channeled his anger at whatever lay ahead.

He brought his arms down and aimed his hands at the enemy.

The clouds overhead opened, bringing forth a bolt of lightning, which crept and crackled across the air and branched off again and again until the clouds were lit up once again.

It left nothing in its wake. Ship after ship crossed its path, until the nearest dozen or so had caught alight.

Screams of terror and pain mixed in with the roaring of flames, as the mainland soldiers on the damaged vessels flung themselves overboard, hoping to escape the fire. The reflection of this unthinkable carnage lit up the sea a fiery orange. It looked like it was boiling. Angry.

When it was done, he sunk onto the ground beside

Eryn, completely spent.

All the anger that had seared him from within all these years, all the vengeance he had plotted since Kelly's initial disappearance, had come together. All this ugliness had culminated in this one moment.

He'd had his revenge. He had made *someone* pay.

And now, he had nothing more to give.

The last thing he saw was something he could not explain. Mainland soldiers, flailing and fighting for their lives, as they were torn to shreds by wild animals that had made their way into the water from the island. Wolves, bears, lynxes and more, all trained to kill.

He sighed deeply as he slipped into oblivion. What a strange place this was. Where animals did these people's bidding just like that. Without magic controlling them.

———•♦•———

E ryn couldn't see properly. Her surroundings, though vaguely familiar, were hazy. Like everything was still covered under the thick mist Ferris had conjured.

She was still on those same fortifications as a moment ago. Her bow was still drawn, with an arrow waiting to hit its aim. She could no longer see the ships, or the flashes of light of the enemy's mysterious weapons.

Where had they gone?

Forget that, where had her own people gone?

Eryn realized now that it was silent all around. Only the distant crash of waves could be heard, along with the sea winds blowing around the towers of the castle behind her. There was not even a whisper in the air otherwise. No clanging of weapons or distant flaps of enemy sails. No cries of wounded men, or whistles of arrows in the air.

She was completely alone.

It made no sense. Just a second ago, she had been fighting for her life with Ferris by her side.

She'd done the needful without hesitation; this time she hadn't failed Rhea or her training. Every arrow had hit exactly where she intended. Many enemy soldiers had fallen thanks to her.

Or had she imagined all of that?

Perhaps the fight never happened.

No, no, no! That cannot be!

Eryn called out into the silence. But no matter how hard she tried, her voice failed to make a sound.

Had she lost her mind?

A shooting pain traveled through her chest, taking her breath away, in the front and straight out the back. Eryn reached for the exact spot and rubbed to soothe the pain away. Still, her chest was so tight she couldn't breathe freely.

She let go and looked down at her hand.

In this gray, hazy world, she saw a first spot of color.

Her palm was covered in red. Blood red.

She cried out again, silently. It was no use.

Eryn stumbled, looking for someone, anyone, to help. But she was still alone, with nothing but the sea and the sky and this desolate bit of castle wall to keep her company.

Just at that moment, she was struck again, from the back this time, and sunk onto her knees.

Had she fallen in battle? Was this the end?

Finally, a sound managed to pass her lips as she whimpered in pain. It wasn't so much the injury that had hurt her. Her suffering went a lot deeper.

Regret.

For the life she would no longer get to live. The love she had denied herself, even though she realized now how much she craved it all along.

CHAPTER TWELVE

Upon opening his eyes, it took Ferris a few minutes to find his bearings. He sat up straight and had a look around. Somehow, he had ended up on an open ground near the Drawbridge that led into the castle, though the wall where his last memories placed him was still within view down below.

The battle was over. Fragments of charred wood floated in the water surrounding the island, along with more bodies than he had the courage to count.

It was carnage.

But it seemed that the worst of the battle was now over. There were no more ships as far as the eye could see. The invaders must have retreated.

"I've got a live one," someone called out.

Ferris turned to see who had said that, but he wasn't sure. Soldiers with only minor injuries, and people he assumed to be servants and workers of the castle, flitted back and forth, trying to attend to as many fallen as possible. Hardly a soul was left unscathed after the battle.

The stench of sweat and blood hung heavily in the air. It was enough to make lesser men sick, but not Ferris. This wasn't the first time he had endured horrors such as these.

He tried to get up, though his limbs were not yet cooperating with him. As he sunk back down onto the damp grass, he noticed a row of a dozen or so lifeless forms, covered in white sheets, just off to his right.

Fear gripped his heart. Was Eryn among these bodies?

Had she been discarded here, while the attendees focused on those casualties whom they could actually help?

The thought of her, alone among the dead, was enough to startle him into action. He stumbled onto his feet and began his search. Frantically he lifted sheet after sheet, only to be faced with numerous faces of soldiers she did not recognize. Interspersed among them were several wild animals as well. It was bizarre how on an island with seemingly no animal life except a handful of eagles, suddenly a whole bunch of wildlife had fallen in battle.

Yet Eryn was nowhere to be found.

"Eryn!" he called out.

His heart raced and his vision went black for a moment as he continued to limp around the mossy plateau. But when he was finally approached, it wasn't *her* face he saw.

"Not so fast," another female voice snapped.

He paused and found Rhea sitting on the ground. A familiar maidservant kneeling by her side was quickly and efficiently cleaning a nasty-looking burn on Rhea's arm. Ferris recognized her as Bree, the woman who had prepared his quarters for him the day before.

"Where is Eryn?" Ferris insisted.

Rhea glared up at him. "Forget Eryn. I knew we couldn't trust you. I knew it from the start!"

Ferris frowned. What was she trying to say? How could

he forget Eryn, when she was the first and last thing on his mind right now?

"You had one job to do. *One* job! Keep us hidden, so that we could move unseen and strike at the enemy until they retreated in fear. Instead, you exposed us and damn near burned my ship down!"

Ferris opened his mouth in protest.

"Shut it!" Rhea interjected. "I'd rather cut off my ears than hear any more of the poison you spew. You think you can convince everyone, but you can no longer lie to me. I see through you, warlock!"

By now Bree had finished tying the bandage around Rhea's arm and moved away to see to someone else. Immediately, Rhea got up and glared at him with a menacing look in her eye. She meant business.

The memories of his last moments before passing out came back to Ferris. Yes, obviously he had failed to hold up his end of the bargain. As soon as he heard Eryn's cry, he'd allowed himself to become distracted. That's when the fog had dissipated.

But that had never been his intent! And it looked like the enemy had retreated anyway, despite his failure.

"I'm so sorry," Ferris mumbled. He was. But what he was most sorry for was that Eryn had been hit. His magic had failed to keep her safe. And Rhea still hadn't told him what exactly happened to her or where she was.

"You will be," Rhea said. "Guards! Take this prisoner

away and lock him somewhere where no one will think to look for him!"

"No! How was I supposed to know you were on one of the ships!" Ferris protested.

"What did you think, that I had slept through the whole battle like a coward? It's only obvious I'd be out there, fighting!" Rhea countered. "Just how your kind managed to win the mainland from us, I'll never understand."

It really had come as a surprise to him that Rhea had fought in this battle along with everyone else. Such a thing was unheard of for someone of her status, at least on the mainland. Then again, the mainland didn't have female fighters or generals either.

"At least tell me where Eryn is?" Ferris insisted.

Rhea scoffed. "Why do you care? You'll never see her again."

Ferris stumbled over his own feet as two men, each at least a foot-and-a-half taller than him, dragged him through the Drawbridge and into the castle.

He'd walked this same route before, on the day of his first arrival on Black Mountain.

It felt like a lifetime ago, even though at the most only two days had passed. And after all that he'd been through, he was a prisoner again.

Thankfully, he didn't get as far as the dungeons before his escort was intercepted by a welcome sight.

"Kelly!" Ferris called out. "Please tell these guys to let

me go."

Kelly's already tense expression turned to anger. "What's the meaning of this? Where are you taking him?"

The guards stopped in their tracks and started to fumble their words. Ferris shook his head and took over the conversation.

"We have the esteemed general to thank for that. She has decided that I'm a traitor and deserve to be locked up," he explained.

Kelly shot the guards a nasty glance. "You're dismissed!"

Then she focused on Ferris again. "Rhea did this? Wouldn't be the first time."

He limbered up his arms and wrists from where the guards had held onto him. "Never mind all that. Where is Eryn?"

Kelly's face fell again. "Oh. You don't know?"

Ferris slowly shook his head as the worst possible scenarios started to play in his mind.

"Right," Kelly mumbled. "I'll take you to her."

———◆———

"How is she?" Ferris asked.

Kelly's expression had told him previously already that it was bad news.

"Please tell me she'll make it," he added. He could not explain how he had developed such strong feelings for her in such a short time. If he lost her, now.... He couldn't bear to think about it.

Kelly shook her head. "There is no way of knowing. Frankly, I haven't seen anything like this before."

"How do you mean?" Ferris looked down at Eryn's motionless body. She was so still it looked like she was simply asleep. Except for the blood-soaked bandage wrapped around her chest, that was.

"Any fever?" Ferris asked, as he leaned down and placed his hand over Eryn's forehead.

Her skin was cold to the touch. He flinched and pulled away.

"They don't get fevers," Kelly said. "They're not like you and me. They don't get sick. They don't heal like we do either. It's much faster."

Although her words were hopeful, her tone didn't match.

"What normally happens? When someone is injured like this?" he asked.

Kelly placed her hand on his arm. "This isn't a normal injury, Ferris. I don't know how to explain it, really."

He turned to face her and look her in the eye. "Kelly. Just be honest with me."

His throat had all but closed up. For so many years he'd had only vengeance on his mind. He'd never cared for anyone else but Kelly. And now, the first other person he'd actually felt something for was on the brink of death.

"I think the first arrow hit her close to her heart. Her

body can't recover as normal, at least not yet. And her mind…."

"What's wrong with her mind?" Ferris asked.

"Normally when someone is passed out, I can still enter their thoughts. She's unreachable to me. Almost like she's stuck in her own consciousness somewhere."

Ferris sank down beside Eryn's bed and kept on staring at her. Her chest was still moving up and down with shallow breaths. Her cheeks still had the faintest hint of color.

Eryn was still here. If these people indeed had extraordinary healing abilities, perhaps she'd get out of it on her own. Had fate led him here, onto this island, only to lose the first woman he'd ever truly loved? And he hadn't even had the chance to tell her so. Surely, life couldn't be so cruel?

"But if she hasn't passed yet, surely she has already begun to heal?"

Kelly carefully picked up the bandage on Eryn's chest and peered underneath.

"Maybe…. But we need both mind as well as body in order to function. If she can't find her way back…."

A sharp knock on the door interrupted the two of them.

Kelly looked up. "General Rhea."

"I've come to check on Eryn," the general said, but then let her gaze linger on Ferris for an uncomfortable few seconds.

"What's *he* doing here?" she asked.

Kelly straightened herself. "I found out about your little scheme, Rhea. He's not going to be your prisoner, no matter what you say. Ferris is assisting me with Eryn's care."

Ferris ignored the two women and kept on watching Eryn's chest rise and fall. As long as she could breathe, there was still hope.

Beside him, Rhea leaned down over Eryn as well. "This doesn't look right."

Kelly joined them.

"I know it doesn't. There's something wrong with her that we haven't encountered before," Kelly said.

Rhea took Kelly by the hand and took her aside. Ferris could only watch as the two women spoke just out of his earshot. He couldn't be bothered to eavesdrop; he had other things on his mind.

Don't you die on me now, Eryn!

What was going on in that head of hers? He would give anything to exchange his powers with Kelly right now to find out. Perhaps he could try to decipher the mystery somehow, and help her find her way back to reality.

The door creaked open again, and yet another person entered. Ferris thought he recognized this guy from the Council meeting, though he hadn't seen him since.

"What's going on? And what's *he* doing here?" The man glared at Ferris, who merely sighed in response. Was this how it was going to go now? Every single person who burst in here seemed more interested in why Ferris was here, rather than working out how to help Eryn.

"Yorrick. We've got it under control," Kelly intervened.

"It doesn't look like it. Not with him here!"

Ferris felt his temper rise again. Did this man have some claim on Eryn which Ferris did not know about? And if so, where was *he* during the battle? Where was *he* when Eryn had needed him the most?

No, Ferris thought to himself. *If anyone has a right to be here, it's me. Not this other guy!*

"Mind yourself!" Rhea snapped as well now. "Eryn needs rest, not your drama."

Finally, Ferris could agree on something Rhea said.

"I only came to check—" the other man, Yorrick, explained.

"Stop it! I know very well what you came here for. Why don't you leave my people alone and check on your own injured? You must have some yourself."

Yorrick turned red, and for a moment Ferris thought it was going to turn into an altercation. But Rhea's authority won out this time.

They all watched as Yorrick left and closed the door behind him.

"That man is going to drive me insane one of these days," Rhea complained, then composed herself as she spotted Ferris staring at her.

"You're lucky your sister wants you here," she told him.

Ferris shrugged. "I guess I *am* lucky that way." *Especially since Kelly is queen, and you're not.* "But we do still have to figure out a way to help Eryn."

Rhea chewed on her bottom lip for a moment. She might hate Ferris, but she obviously did care for Eryn.

"We should consult the Elders," Rhea concluded finally.

Kelly nodded.

Ferris had no idea what that meant exactly, but it seemed to be their best hope.

CHAPTER THIRTEEN

When Eryn awoke, she was high up in the sky with no recollection of how she got there. Night had started to fall, and the clouds that surrounded her were only lit up with the faint moonlight that filtered through the haze. She circled around and headed back the same way where she had just come from.

The fog down below was still dense, making it almost impossible for Eryn to see the ground. The spires of the highest tower of the castle were the only thing that was clearly visible to her.

Just how long she had been flying for, she did not know.

She stretched her wings as wide as they would go, allowing the breeze to carry her. With the right amount of wind, it was almost effortless to fly this high.

Effortless, and blissfully quiet.

A little too quiet.

She dove down a little, and headed right for the thickest part of the fog. Still, she could detect no movement down below. Even at night, there was always someone, some guard or soldier, patrolling the castle walls.

Her very own squad ought to be around here somewhere, seeking out incoming threats from the sky.

But there was no one.

Not a single sound could be heard, save for the sea and he wind itself, along with the flapping of her wings.

A sense of doom overcame her. Something was not right.

There was a tightness in her chest she could not explain. It made it hard to breathe. She closed her eyes for a moment, when a flash of a memory came to her.

Blood.

Pain.

Darkness.

Eryn's heart sped up instantly, but her breathing couldn't catch up. The tightness on her lungs worsened.

What happened to the battle she'd been in? Who won? Who lost?

What *was* this place and how did she get here?

The view beneath her changed. The once mossy hill on which the castle stood turned ashen, as the outer walls of the building began to crumble.

She averted her gaze from the nightmarish vision, only to see a dangerous orange glow in the water.

The sea had changed too. Suddenly it looked like the water had caught fire. A terrible heat rose up from it, singeing the tips of her feathers.

Eryn quickly turned back, hoping to reach the View Point before she ran out of time and air.

She had barely made it close to the correct tower when she was knocked back by a piercing sensation in her breast. She'd been hit by something, but what?

As she looked down at herself, she lost all sense of direction. Her wings refused to cooperate any longer and she started to fall, faster and faster, rotating on her own axis as she crashed.

She never felt the impact.

Instead, she kept on falling and falling, until a familiar voice called out to her from somewhere beyond her view.

"Eryn!"

She tried to turn around, but her body was no longer able. *Ferris? Where are you?*

———◆———

"**I**s it working?" Rhea asked.

Ferris frowned, but did not open his eyes or reply to her.

She's so impatient, he complained to Kelly.

That's nothing new, Kelly responded in his head. *Focus.*

He tried harder. The little veins on the side of his head began to throb and he felt a headache coming on.

But that was nothing compared to what Eryn was going through. He would endure this little discomfort if it meant there was a chance of helping her.

Beside them, Uri cleared his throat and mumbled something to Rhea which Ferris could only partially understand.

Something about focus and distraction. Rhea grumbled an unintelligible response.

Finally, it was quiet. He inhaled deeply. The battle had all but wiped him out. Ordinarily he would have waited before attempting to perform magic again, but right now, there wasn't any time. Uri had pretty much confirmed it earlier.

If Eryn was stuck in her own version of purgatory, they had only so long to try and get her out before her mind would be lost forever.

Try to speak to her while you do it. Maybe that'll help wake her mind to your presence.

Kelly's suggestion didn't make much sense to him, but she was the mind-reading expert here; he wasn't.

As his consciousness emerged from his physical body, he could clearly see everything and everyone around him.

"Eryn, come back to us," Ferris said. As soon as he'd spoken those few words, he saw something unusual in her: a shadowy being clinging to her damaged body, which stirred at the sound of his voice.

Rhea scoffed. "This is stupid. I'm leaving. Someone, call me if this sorcery works."

Ferris breathed in and out, as deeply and slowly as he could, to maintain his fragile state of being. Suspended between life and death, he felt his body growing weaker and weaker.

"It's probably best if we all leave," Kelly whispered. "This is going to be difficult enough without all the distractions."

Uri mumbled something in agreement, and soon after,

the two of them left the room. Only Eryn and Ferris remained.

He approached her and reached out for her hand. The way Kelly had explained it, she didn't have to leave her body to join another's mind. She merely heard and transmitted thoughts. Perhaps that was why she had no luck using her powers on Eryn. Her mind was too confused to allow her in.

The only thing left to try was for him to enter her, like he had done with much simpler creatures so many times before.

Out on the battlefield he had performed feats he had never thought possible. A little lighting strike was all he had achieved in the past.

Perhaps it was the thought of losing her that had sparked a greater power within him? Was there any greater motivator than fear?

Chances were that he would fail, and she would slip away. But how could he live with himself if he didn't at least try? So what if he went down with her? She was worth the sacrifice.

He gave it everything he had, and forced his soul to enter her.

Surprisingly, there was little resistance, but it wasn't an easy transition. All her pain, he felt it now. The wound in her chest was severe. Just how she could bear it, he did not know.

Was she even still in here with him?

Eryn! he thought. *Eryn, please, can you hear me?*

He tried to move, but her body wouldn't budge. He was just a helpless passenger of an incapacitated body.

Of course, moving her physical form wouldn't achieve anything. It was her mind he had to try and reach.

Eryn, damn it. Don't leave me!

The shadow he'd spotted earlier appeared again, right above her body. Strangely, it wasn't human; it was shaped like an eagle as it was trying to leave her body. He reached for its wing and held on for dear life.

Spirit to spirit, he was able to sense her fear as if it were his own.

Eryn, listen to me. You have to come back. You're not done yet with this life.

The form flapped and struggled, as it fought furiously to get away from him. With his last shred of energy, he was able to subdue it.

I'm dying, Ferris! I've been hit by the enemy! All is lost. The battle is lost.

Ferris' heartbeat surged as he sensed her response.

You're just confused. Your body has already started to heal. And we won the battle shortly after you went down.

The shadow transformed. What was once an eagle had turned into a human again. Finally, his words were getting through to her. Even the fear he'd sensed in her had subsided.

Where are you? Why am I all alone?

You're not alone, Eryn. I'm here to get you back.

As her spirit settled back into her body, Ferris was immediately expelled into the empty space between them. He exhaled slowly and focused on getting back into his own physical form.

He got up in a rush to check Eryn. Her skin was still cold, and her eyes remained closed.

Still, he'd communicated with her. He'd brought her back to her body. Surely it wasn't all for nothing?

Ferris rushed to the door, where Kelly and the others were still waiting around.

"Sis, something's happened. Please go and see if you can communicate with her now."

———◆———

Eryn awoke with a gasp and sat up straight. Everything hurt. Every breath, every movement. She immediately regretted moving at all.

When she opened her eyes, she expected to see the foggy place again. Whether in the sky or on the ground, she had always found herself in the same place. And the ordeal had always ended the same way, with what she assumed to be her own death.

But she was inside the castle, in her own room now. And there was no fog to be seen.

She wasn't alone anymore either. Surrounding her were a multitude of familiar faces.

There was Uri, who smiled down on her. "Welcome back, young Eryn."

With that same stabbing pain she'd dreamt about continuing to pierce her chest, she did not feel particularly young.

"Eryn, how do you feel?" Rhea asked. She'd never seen Rhea look this concerned before.

Eryn simply shook her head in response. Talking would hurt.

Honestly? She felt worse than she'd ever felt before.

Then, turning her head further to the right, she saw a more unexpected sight. Ferris, whose wide smile could not disguise just how terrible he looked. Had he been injured as well?

"Don't talk yet. It's alright," Ferris spoke softly.

Eryn sighed and slowly lay back down on her back. *Oh, it hurts.*

"I think let's allow her to rest. Now that she's back with us, she'll heal up fast," Uri said.

Eryn closed her eyes and tried to find a more comfortable breathing pattern. She was unsuccessful.

Footsteps shuffled away from her bed, and the door opened and closed. She sensed that everyone had left. Everyone except one person, that was.

Eryn opened her eyes again and noticed that Ferris had sat down on a chair beside her bed. Although she couldn't voice it, she was glad he was here.

She could see in his eyes that he had gone through a

fair amount of pain himself, though he seemed to be mostly intact physically. When the time was right, she would find out everything she'd missed during her absence.

He did not ask her anything, neither did she speak. But instinctively she knew that she was here now because of him somehow.

And his body had clearly paid a heavy price to make it happen.

Ferris leaned over and took her hand. It made her feel weird, but in a nice way.

He cared. Just why and how she had deserved this affection, she did not know. If she'd followed her orders rather than hesitated, she would have killed him in his sleep shortly after his capture. By all accounts, he shouldn't be alive today, yet here he was.

And words could not express how grateful she was for that.

CHAPTER FOURTEEN

ryn's recovery was lighting fast, at least compared to what Ferris was used to.

Within a day, she was able to talk, and two days later, she was almost back on her feet.

An injury such as hers would have killed most humans; if not on the spot, then within hours.

Kelly was right. The islanders were different. They didn't get sick, and they healed extraordinarily quickly.

And as it turned out, that wasn't the only difference between them and mainlanders like Ferris himself. He was shocked to learn the reason for the strange animal appearances around the islands. The eagles overhead, and the wolves and bears he'd seen during the aftermath of the battle, were the islanders themselves.

And that eagle he had tried to possess on his first day had been Eryn all along.

It was yet another reason for Ferris to admire her.

And luckily, the feeling appeared to be mutual. She seemed to be enjoying his company, judging by the way her eyes lit up whenever he came and saw her.

But he'd been cautious not to get ahead of himself. They'd become friends, even confidantes. But he knew he wanted so much more.

After getting past the initial awkwardness between

them, Eryn had opened up to him.

They talked for hours every day, learning everything there was to know about each other.

Ferris told her about the battle, and all that had happened since. He'd tried to omit Rhea's attempt to imprison him again, but soon realized he was unable to keep too many secrets from her.

Thankfully she was in good spirits and could have a little laugh about it all.

One morning, three or four days after the battle, Ferris decided it was time to have a *real* conversation. Finally, he would know if she truly felt as he did, or if this friendship was doomed to remain only that.

"Morning, Eryn," Ferris greeted her as he entered the room.

She was sitting up in bed already, with a bowl of soup resting on her lap.

"Morning." She smiled brightly, and his nerves subsided a little.

He sat down on the chair at her bedside and folded his hands. The past seven years might have taught him a lot, but nothing that would be of use now. He hadn't the faintest idea how to proposition a woman. Worse still, he didn't know if the customs here were different.

Should he have brought her a token of some sort, to show his affection?

"You look troubled. Is something wrong?" Eryn asked.

"No, no… Nothing is wrong." Ferris' tone sounded unconvincing even to his own ears.

Now or never!

"That day, during the battle, I made a promise to myself," Ferris began.

Eryn put her spoon down and focused solely on him.

"I said to myself, if we make it through to the end alive, I'm going to ask you something."

He leaned over and took her hand. It was warm and soft, and the feel of her skin against his made his heart beat even faster.

"Ask me what?" Eryn whispered.

The mood in the room had changed. The air had grown heavy with tension. He swallowed his fears and blurted it all out.

"Would you become my wife?"

Eryn's eyes widened as she was stunned into silence.

"I would give you a ring, or some other token to show I'm serious, but I have nothing to give but myself. I promise you'll have my loyalty for as long as I'm alive," Ferris said.

His voice had gone flat. How could it be that he'd faced off against any number of enemies, and yet speaking to this one woman had sent him into a blind panic?

He'd never been afraid of injury or death, but these stakes were higher. If Eryn refused him, he knew he would suffer gravely.

"It's not possible," Eryn stammered and pulled her

hand away. "How could we possibly do this?"

Ferris' heart all but stopped. He glanced at her, and found that she already had tears in her eyes. How could she not be interested? Had he misinterpreted the way she looked at him?

"You're…" Eryn took a deep breath. "You're the queen's brother!"

Ferris didn't know how to respond to that. What bearing did his relation to Kelly have in all of this? Finally, it dawned on him what she meant.

"I'm nobody," he said. "I'm a liar, a thief and a murderer. I almost destroyed your people in my search for revenge. Reject me on that basis, not because of Kelly."

Eryn sniffled. "But you saved us. You saved me."

"I was only trying to undo the wrong I'd caused."

Eryn stared at him. The sudden silence between them threatened to overwhelm. He wanted to scream, just to break it. But he didn't; instead he waited for her to speak first.

"I'm not worthy," Eryn finally said.

Ferris pressed his lips together, and maintained eye contact. She seemed to truly believe that. How could she possibly be serious? This woman, who was a million times better than him, was hung up on his supposed status? He hadn't earned that kind of consideration. And Kelly herself didn't care; she'd just seemed amused by the idea when she first noticed.

"You're wrong," Ferris said. "I'm the one who's unworthy."

For days he'd watched her recover, but right now she looked more pained than she had through the worst of it. The outcome of their conversation was causing her as much grief as it was him. And all of it was completely unnecessary.

"Will you just tell me one thing?" Ferris asked. "If it were just you and me in this world, nobody else. What would your answer be?"

"That's obvious," Eryn whispered with a tremble in her voice. "I'd say yes."

Ferris stretched out his hand and watched as Eryn placed hers in his palm again. She shivered slightly as he closed his fingers gently around hers.

"Then forget about all the rest of it," Ferris said. "Kelly doesn't mind, and she can handle anyone who objects."

"But…"

Ferris placed his finger on Eryn's lips. "Trust me?"

She nodded. "I do."

"Nobody will come between us. I promise," he said.

For a change, he wasn't bluffing or exaggerating. He would move heaven and earth to get what he wanted. If he had to fight everyone on this island, from the king down to that irritating man who'd made a scene while Eryn was still unconscious, he would do it without hesitation.

She looked up at him in silence. The despair he'd just seen in her eyes was slowly dissipating. Perhaps he was getting through to her.

"Why me?" she asked. "Neither am I as good a fighter as Rhea, nor am I as pretty as the mainland girls."

Ferris smiled briefly. "Because I've never met anyone like you. You're perfect just the way you are."

Eryn smiled through her tears and bit her lip. "I've never met anyone like you either."

———— ◆ ————

Eryn couldn't believe her luck. Every day, Ferris had come to spend time with her and to care for her. She had cherished their moments together, even if she assumed it would all come to an end once she was fully recovered.

Somewhere in the back of her mind she'd always wondered, what if this was something more than just friendship? But she'd rejected the notion as quickly as it had come up.

She wasn't from one of the prominent Black Isle families like Rhea and even Yorrick. She was a commoner.

Why would he care for her like that?

But he had surprised her, despite all of her protests and concerns.

"You're perfect just the way you are." These words continued to ring in her ears, moments after he had first said them.

She was overwhelmed by the realization that all the

things she'd been trying not to think about, he'd been thinking too. The attraction she'd felt from the start, he had felt it too.

That's why he had joined her on the battlefield, when he could have performed his magic anywhere and not been so dangerously close to the action.

And it was also the reason he had avenged her injury and burned down half of the mainland's fleet of ships. After all that, he had mustered the last of his reserves to try and bring her back from the dead. She'd seen in his eyes just how close to the brink he had come. All for her.

What more could she ask for in a mate? And if the queen didn't object, then...

"Do you really think it's possible?" Eryn asked.

"Anything is possible now."

He leaned over and placed his hand on the side of her face. His touch made her cheeks burn up, and caused her breaths to quicken.

"Unless Rhea tries to arrest me again," he added.

"Don't joke," she said.

He was so close to her now, his heady perfume stirred up those same desires she'd had all along. Instinct was threatening to take over. All the things she knew her body craved; they were now within reach.

"Prove it with a kiss," she whispered.

He didn't need any more encouragement than that.

The moment their lips touched for the very first time, she knew there was no turning back. All the tension, all the yearning she'd felt, it was all about to be unleashed.

It was the animal side of her, taking over. Just what she'd been afraid of all this time, she could no longer remember.

It felt so right; his flesh against hers.

She got onto her knees on the edge of her bed, and pulled him closer by his hand until they were more evenly matched. The taste of his lips was intoxicating.

He pulled away just enough to speak. "Tell me if it hurts."

His breath tickled her face, which sent her heart racing even faster.

"My wound healed days ago," Eryn said. "Don't worry about me."

She wrapped her arms around him and pulled him against her. This was what she had craved. It was the sort of passion that made you stupid. She'd never understood it until this very moment.

His body was firm to the touch, muscular like her own, but also very different. His skin was so smooth, she couldn't stop running her hands over him as they continued to make out.

What a beautiful man he was. He didn't have the rough edges of some of the islanders. Only a few scars adorned his skin. She touched every single one of them with the tip of her finger.

Ferris. It made her happy to say his name.

Now that she had given herself permission to feel, she was overcome with so many emotions at once. She could laugh, or cry, or both at the same time.

Was this how it felt to love?

Eryn had no idea that things would get more intense still.

Ferris joined her on the bed and guided her down on her back. His hands were on an exploratory journey of their own. Her side, her hips, her stomach and her breasts, he caressed her all over.

As he looked down on her, Eryn noticed his eyes had turned almost black with lust. She could smell the change in him, heard the racing of his heart as his body was overcome by desire.

It made her want him more.

Everything about him seemed designed to turn her on.

Ferris climbed on top of her and allowed his hand to travel downward, pushing her nightgown out of the way.

Eryn moaned and raised her hips to meet his touch.

She'd never done this before, but her body was telling her exactly what was needed.

As he lowered himself on top of her, she dug her fingernails into his shoulders. His manhood pressed up against her thigh.

"Oh please, don't hold back," she whispered impatiently.

Ferris paused and stared into her eyes. The look in his gaze was wild. He wanted this as much as she did. Nobody could stop them now.

He let his fingers slip in between her legs.

She gasped as he found a spot most sensitive. All the pleasure in the world couldn't compare to what she felt right now.

She forced her own hand in between the two of them and touched him intimately. He shuddered as she tightened her fingers around his shaft.

Although it was her first time, she never hesitated. She guided him inside of her and cried out in pleasure as her body adjusted to him.

Just like that, they had become one.

Eryn's mind went blank. Not a doubt remained.

This was right. This was just. Nobody could take this away from her; she wouldn't allow it anymore.

Ferris rocked back and forth into her. They were different species, human and islander, but in this moment, they were exactly the same.

It did not take long for either of them to reach their peak. After trying to contain this passion for so long, their bodies simply let go.

Eryn was overcome with a wave of pleasure so strong, it knocked the wind out of her.

On top, Ferris groaned to a halt almost at the same time. He shuddered and strained as his seed flooded into her.

That's how they remained, until the fog of ecstasy lifted

enough for them to realize what had just happened.

"Well, that was unexpected," Ferris spoke as he fell back onto the bed.

Eryn chuckled. "I blame the animal in me."

"If that is your excuse, then what do I blame?" Ferris stretched out his arm and pulled Eryn's still naked body against him.

She had no answer for him; instead of talking more she rested her head on his shoulder and closed her eyes.

How warm he was. Meanwhile her own body was cool underneath the thin layer of sweat that their union had produced.

Could it be that this was her life now? He was hers and she was his, and they would sleep and wake like this, lying body to body, every night for the rest of their lives?

She wished for nothing more.

<h1 style="text-align:center">CHAPTER FIFTEEN</h1>

———•◆•———

Days had passed since Ferris had first confessed his feelings to Eryn. Their relationship was progressing faster than he could have ever anticipated.

Now that she was fully recovered, they had become even closer, physically as well as emotionally.

But one thing still stood in the way of their future. One thing which had been playing on Ferris' mind since waking after the battle.

Despite everything, he'd failed to keep them safe.

His outburst on the battlefield had torched a bunch of the royal navy's ships, sure. But not all of them.

And although they had retreated for now, Ferris was certain a single setback like this wouldn't discourage King Harrold from trying again. The mainland army would be back, and perhaps the next time, a bit of fog might not be enough to thwart their attack.

The islanders were powerful and had many talents, but they weren't cannon-proof. Their weaponry was severely lacking as well.

He could not have any more deaths on his conscience. No, Ferris owed it to Eryn, as well as Kelly and Finlay, to redeem himself.

So, one morning he decided to discuss the matter with

King Broc.

With every passing day, the threat grew bigger. It was only a matter of time before they would be under attack again.

"My King," Ferris addressed him. "I'd like a word."

Broc greeted him with a pat on the back. "I've never had a brother-in-law before, but I'm quite sure such formalities are not required among family. Just call me Broc."

It was a relief that Broc was becoming more welcoming, but still, the ruler of the Black Isles struck an imposing figure.

"Very well…. Broc." It was odd, addressing him that way.

"What can I do for you, Ferris?" the king asked.

He was in an unusually jovial mood today. Perhaps it was still the thrill of victory.

"I mean to discuss a proposition," Ferris began.

Broc's expression sobered up. "Continue."

"As you know I was sent here as an envoy to King Harrold of the mainland. He then sent his navy after us to complete the invasion."

"Yes, and you fought them off almost single-handedly as I hear it."

Ferris shook his head. "Conjecture and exaggeration. I did what I could at the time. But I doubt we've seen the last of the mainland."

"You mean, they will attack again? Despite running

away the last time, like cowards?" Broc raised an eyebrow.

"Well, I have an idea to avoid such a scenario. If you're willing to make a couple of concessions."

"Carry on."

"The Reaping, as you call it. King Harrold is using at as an excuse to motivate his army," Ferris said.

Broc scratched his beard, then looked down at Ferris again. "You mean to say that if we do away with the Reaping, his soldiers will have no more reason to fight?"

Ferris nodded. "That's exactly what I'm saying."

"We can't afford another battle. Not this quickly." Broc paced the hall as he spoke.

"I know." Ferris folded his arms in an attempt to look more confident in his plan.

The king paused and studied Ferris' face. "Are you sure this will work?"

It's going to have to. I've got nothing else. "Absolutcly."

"Alright…. What's the other concession?" Broc asked.

"Let me have the prisoners. I'll return them as a gesture of goodwill."

***

"Funny, that you would turn on your own people so quickly!" King Harrold sneered, as Ferris entered the throne hall.

Ferris stared the man down. King or no king, he wasn't going to accept insults from anyone. And he certainly wasn't going to show weakness, not when he had so much riding on this moment.

"And to think I believed your story. About your missing sister, who had been chosen in the last lottery. My senses must be failing me in my advanced age that I did not predict your deceit!" King Harrold ranted on.

"Trust me, you've seen nothing much of me yet," Ferris countered.

"Apparently! I should have you executed where you stand!"

"You could try, but your men would fall before they even got close to me. Or did you not hear about what happened during the battle?" Ferris straightened himself and continued to glare directly at the king. He knew very well that he was breaking every single rule of protocol, and yet he did not care.

A murmur passed through the small group of royal advisors. Some of them shuffled uncomfortably from one foot onto the other.

Good. They *ought* to be afraid of him.

The king himself, however, remained unfazed. Either he was completely uninformed, or he knew more about Ferris and his magic than he let on.

But Ferris had come here with a clear goal in mind. If they called his bluff, so be it. He was willing to make the sacrifice.

"I haven't come here to hear your judgement. I'm more than content with the choices I have made," Ferris said.

What a joke this was. After the short time Ferris had

spent on Black Mountain, he'd come to find the ways of the mainlanders to be ludicrous in comparison.

On one side there was a king who had clearly earned his place, through just rule as well as prowess in battle. Yet here sat nothing but a frail old man, and yet everyone treated him with reverence he did not deserve. What had *he* ever done for his people?

"Then what exactly are you doing here?" King Harrold folded his arms across his chest and tapped his foot impatiently.

Ferris looked at him in disgust.

How had this king ever helped Ferris and Kelly when they were growing up in West Hythe? Theirs was a life lived in poverty, with barely enough food to get by. And as soon as Ferris left to earn a little money, Kelly had been taken in the lottery.

The villagers had no idea what would happen to her, neither did they care. For all they know, she had died the day they left her on the beach.

It was pure luck that Broc had taken her in and treated her with more kindness than her own people had shown her. She had arrived in a better place, purely by chance.

Meanwhile, this supposed ruler had a limitless supply of food and all the shiny trinkets money could buy, while his advisers did nothing but brown nose him. When had he ever seen pain or sacrifice? He'd sent his soldiers off to fight a hopeless war at sea, for what?

To stop the lottery? This charlatan cared nothing about the lottery. He was in it to expand his territory.

This king had never done a single thing to deserve Ferris' respect.

"I'm here to warn you to forget about the Black Isles," Ferris spoke in a threatening tone.

Still, the man's arrogant expression remained.

"Or, what? We saw what your barbarian friends had to offer. A few soldiers, easily wiped out if I send in reinforcements." King Harrold snapped his finger to make his point.

Ferris laughed out loud. "Oh, is that what you think? I do believe you have been misinformed. What your men encountered was just a taste of what the Black Isles can unleash. Now that they're expecting a fight, they can summon an army that will put yours to shame. Perhaps question those *loyal* advisors of yours in a bit more detail."

"Are you just going to stand there while this peasant disrespects me?" the king raged. "All of you, what are you here for, exactly? Tell him!"

The small cluster of fancily-dressed men took a moment to confer, until one of them reluctantly stepped forward.

"Your Majesty, although we outnumbered them approximately four-to-one, the enemy fought with such fury, we would need to overwhelm them with troops we simply don't have," the advisor spoke in a trembling voice.

Finally, someone had stepped up against this decrepit

tyrant.

The king stood up from his throne and pointed at the door. "Then go out there and get me some more men!"

"That…. I'm so sorry, Your Majesty, but even the men we currently have aren't willing to go back into battle. Not against this particular enemy."

Ferris simply watched the exchange. He'd expected to have more trouble than this. To threaten and perhaps show everyone a taste of his powers. But it seemed that the advisors were doing his job for him.

"They get a spot of bad weather during a fight and want to run for the hills?" the king raised his fist in the air. "I won't stand for this. Find me braver soldiers, then! And fire the ones we have without pay."

A spot of bad weather. This was the perfect time to teach these people a lesson.

Ferris closed his eyes and inhaled deeply. He visualized the throne room now, with a gust of wind blowing through it and extinguishing all the candles and torches at once.

Gasps and whispers could be heard from his left where the advisors stood. The cold wind tickled the hairs on his arms.

"What's the meaning of this? Stop it, right now!" the king ordered.

He was trying to maintain a brave front, but Ferris could hear fear in his voice.

Ferris opened his eyes and stared right at the king. "It's a dangerous thing, the unknown. I promise that if you face off against the Isles again, you'll encounter things you can't even imagine in your worst nightmares."

The monarch's face had turned a deep crimson. "What do you want?"

"That's all. Peace."

"And what do we get out of it? How do I justify this to the people?" the king asked.

Ferris smiled briefly. *Justify it to the people. As if he gives a damn what ordinary folk think.* "An end to the lottery. The daughters of East and West Hythe will be safe from now on."

Once again, a murmur travelled the small crowd, until the same one who had spoken up earlier approached the king again.

"Your Majesty. We believe this to be a fair deal," he whispered, though he was just loud enough for Ferris to overhear.

"So, do we have an agreement, then?" Ferris asked.

He produced the two identical scrolls Uri had prepared shortly after he'd gotten Broc's blessing. A replacement for the old treaty that had been drawn up so many centuries ago.

The king made a face, but then nodded briefly. "Very well. Prepare my seal."

Ferris watched as another one of the advisors carefully took the scrolls from him, and stamped the royal seal onto both of them, before presenting them to the king to sign. He then rolled them up individually, and handed one back to Ferris.

"You'd better go, before he changes his mind," the man whispered fearfully.

So much fear, all for an old man who possessed neither strength nor talons or fangs. All he had in his favor was the privilege of his birth.

"A good day to you all. Your Majesty." Ferris greeted them with a comically exaggerated bow. Then he left the hall with a spring in his step.

Ferris knew he'd never to return to these lands ever again, and that was fine by him. Like Kelly, he had found a better home.

Rhea would still be skeptical of him, of course, but he could handle that.

With this achievement behind him he could honestly say he had held up his end of the deal. The war he had thrust everyone into—he had undone it as much as he possibly could.

This piece of paper, this symbol, would allow calm to return to the Isles.

And Eryn and he could live out the rest of their lives together, in peace.

EPILOGUE

"And that was the story of how I met your aunt Eryn," Ferris concluded.

The boy's eyes were wide and his lips slightly parted. He had been completely engrossed in every word so far.

"She almost died?" Finlay asked. "And you and my mom had to rescue her from the shadow world in her own mind?"

Ferris nodded. "It's true. You can ask her yourself." Although he had told the story dozens of times by now, that part still stung as though it had happened yesterday.

"I can't believe I missed the entire battle and everything!" Finlay folded his arms in frustration.

"It was for your own safety."

Finlay scoffed. "I can fight, too! Dad has been teaching me how to use a sword."

Ferris chuckled. "I don't doubt it. You'll be a great warrior one day."

"I can't wait to grow up and have adventures of my own. Then, when I come back, I'll be the one to tell you stories." Finlay smiled and Ferris' heart melted.

He was a sweet boy. He could see a lot of Kelly in him, not least because he indeed had the same eyes and the same flaming red hair.

"You'd better. You owe me a good story after all the

ones I've told you already!" Ferris laughed. "But now, I think we can all agree it's bedtime."

"No! Just one more, please, Uncle Ferris?" Finlay complained. They had this same conversation every day. And it always ended the same way.

Ferris shook his head. "You know what to do. Don't make me tell you again."

Finlay sighed and lay down flat in his cot.

"Eyes closed!" Ferris ordered.

Finlay grimaced and shut his eyes so tightly his little face was all scrunched up.

Behind him, Ferris heard the soft creak of an opening door. His senses might not be as powerful as those of the islanders, but Ferris' nose told him exactly who it was.

Her sweet perfume was unmistakable.

"Almost ready here? Broc has called us for a meeting," Eryn said. "Sweet dreams, Finlay!"

Finlay lifted his head. "Good night, Aunt Eryn!"

"You heard the lady. I've got somewhere to be. You be good now and go to sleep."

"Alright then. But tomorrow, you tell me another story."

"Of course. Any thoughts on what story you want to hear?" Ferris asked.

"I want to know how it happened that my mom and I were already here, but you came much later. Will you tell it to me?"

Ferris thought for a moment. "I think that particular

one is best told by your mother herself. You just wait. Once she's back with your little brother or sister, she'll tell you exactly what happened."

Finlay made a face. "She won't tell me. I already asked."

"Don't worry. I'll talk to her. You're a big boy now, so you're ready to hear that story as well."

"You think so?" Finlay asked.

"I know so."

With a reassured smile on his face, Finlay finally settled into his pillow and closed his eyes.

"Ok, Uncle Ferris. Good night."

"Sleep well. Little man." Ferris patted Finlay on the head, then quietly left the room and joined Eryn, who had been waiting in the hallway.

"He's going to sleep now," Ferris explained.

Eryn suppressed a smile. "If I didn't know any better, I would have thought that Ferris, the Great Warlock of the Mainland, had finally met his match. The boy's every wish is your command."

"Ha, if you say so. Though I'd argue that's true for you too."

"What is?" Eryn cocked her head to the side.

She might be tough as nails and a fearsome opponent if you met her on the battlefield. But during these little moments, they were just an ordinary couple, and she was a woman like any other. Ferris cherished this feminine side as much as the warrior in her.

He leaned over and slipped his hand across the nape of her neck. With their lips only an inch or so apart, he whispered those all-important words he knew she wanted to hear.

"Your wish is my command too."

Her eyes fluttered shut as she leaned into him, allowing their lips to touch. This right here made everything worth it. All the pain and suffering they had been through; it was meaningless now that they were together.

What had started out as mere quiet admiration on his side had awoken a burning flame of passion that he'd never expected to feel.

Her body's reaction to his touch proved that their attraction remained mutual.

Ever since he'd met her, he was willing to be a better man. A good husband. A devoted father to their children, should they have them eventually.

He had become all the things his own father had never been. All for her.

It was with great reluctance that he pulled away from their sweet kiss.

Ferris looked into Eryn's eyes and saw that she was smiling.

"What do you say, we'll pick that up later, in peace…. You said something about a meeting with the king?" Ferris asked.

Eryn nodded. "That's right. We shouldn't keep him waiting."

THE END

ABOUT THE AUTHOR

Dear Reader,

Thanks for reading The Warlock's Conquest. In this fourth book in the Shifters of Black Isles series, I bring back someone who was first mentioned all the way at the beginning in Claimed by the King... Ferris, Kelly's younger brother finds his sister missing. Rather than give up on her, he vows revenge and sure enough, seven years later he sails to the Black Isles to get her back, only to find that she isn't in need of rescue at all.

This book was a lot of fun to write, so I hope you've enjoyed it equally as a reader. Ferris' story had been begging to be written since I started the series during the summer of 2018, so hopefully I was able to do him justice with his own book.

I may have only released my first book in 2015, but I'm not new to writing in general. In fact, my mom still tells me to this day about how I would make up stories, and attempt to record them in my clumsy, shaky handwriting from the moment I learned to read and write. From there I went on to write fan fiction and other stuff meant for my own eyes only.

I've always enjoyed stories of the fantastic and paranormal. Vampires, shape shifters, witches and magic, all featured in the books I loved the most, even when I was still growing up. But it wasn't until much later that I got into romance. One of the first writers (an independent author just like me!) I came across was Tina Folsom, via her Scanguards Vampire series. I was hooked. From there I went on to read more paranormal romance until I found a new kind of hero I loved: bear shifters, like the kind written by Milly Taiden, Zoe Chant, and T.S. Joyce. What I love about bears is how they can be all strong and independent, a bit reclusive, and almost grumpy, but they always end up having a heart of gold (plus they tend to know their food, and we all know that a man who can cook is doubly sexy). All that (except for the shifting into a powerful bear) almost exactly describes the sort of man I ended up falling for and marrying in real life, so it's no surprise that this is what I started my publishing career with.

To find out more, check:

LoreleiMoone.com (And why not sign up for the newsletter to be the first to find out about new releases.)

You can also get in touch with me via Facebook (search for Lorelei Moone), or email at info@loreleimoone.com

HAVE YOU MET THE SCOTTISH WEREBEARS?

Before there was Alpha Squad, there were the Scottish Werebears… And if you sign up for Lorelei Moone's mailing list at loreleimoone.com, you get Book 1, Scottish Werebear: An Unexpected Affair absolutely free!

Titles in the Scottish Werebears series include:

An Unexpected Affair

A Dangerous Business

A Forbidden Love

A New Beginning

A Painful Dilemma

A Second Chance

These individual books in the Scottish Werebears series are best read in order. They can also be enjoyed as part of the Scottish Werebear: Complete Collection boxed set.

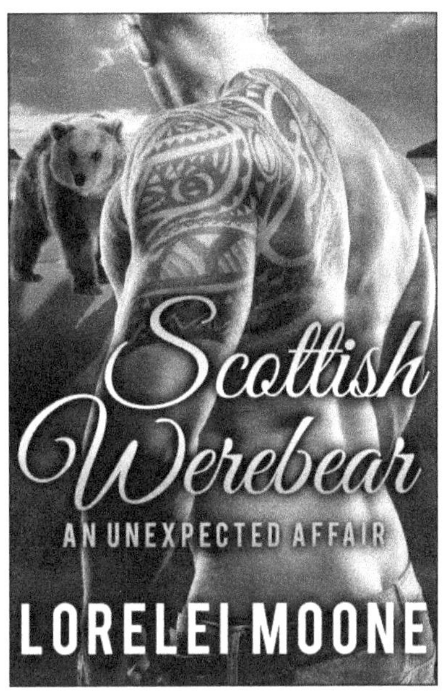

When romance novelist, Clarice Adler, hides herself away in a secluded holiday cottage to finish a book, the last thing she needs is another relationship. Imagine her surprise when she falls head over heels for the man who runs the place. Derek McMillan knows Clarice is his mate, but he's a bear shifter and she's human and the two simply don't mix. They are literally worlds apart; can they find a way to come together?

Get this book for free by joining Lorelei Moone's mailing list at loreleimoone.com!